Bad Brakes
by
Stephen Cohen

Fictional work based on actual WWII events.

The moral right of Stephen Cohen to be identified as the author of this work has been asserted in accordance with the Copyright, Design and Patents Act 1988

Bad Brakes
ISBN 979-8-89778-572-8

Criminality during the war:

Looting was a big problem. The number of bombed properties provided a big temptation to looters. Many were given fines or short prison sentences.

Black market: Many items were sold on the black market without a ration card. If caught selling on the black market, then the punishment could be a fine and imprisonment.

Murder rates increased dramatically during the war. Air raids killed so many people, it was often impossible for the police to investigate all deaths and criminals took advantage of this. Murder carried the death penalty.

Police duties:

Their usual tasks included keeping the peace, dealing with criminals and making sure that the traffic flowed freely in towns and cities.

The Police also had new wartime duties. They had to make sure people obeyed the wartime blackout rules, help the rescue services during and after bombing raids and search for soldiers who had deserted (run away) from the army.

Many police were called *blackout bobbies* because they had to make sure that no light from houses and shops could be seen outside. This was to protect buildings from German bombers flying overhead.

There were not many women police officers.

Dedication

Kell-Mae Matt – Words cannot express how much I have become to rely on this lady. Over the past year we have worked on several projects together and developed not just a great working relationship, but a strong friendship to boot. Thank you, Kelly (My Scribe Taming **Sorceress**) for being my friend and editor. My world is a brighter place with you in it.

CHAPTER ONE

War-Torn Norwich, 1941

The war had changed the city of Norwich, yet life stubbornly persisted. In the city centre, the once vibrant marketplace, now a shadow of its former self, was slowly coming to life as vendors set up their meagre stalls. These days, it wasn't bustling with the variety and abundance it used to hold—rationing and shortages had reduced both goods and customers—but those who remained made the best of what little they had.

DI Brakes watched it all from his regular corner table at the café. He had come to rely on the place as part of his morning routine—tea, a quick survey of the market, and then back to the grind at the station. The war might have slowed down the world around him, but Brakes was always in motion.

Finishing the last sip of his tea, he gathered his things and left the café, intending to head to the station. As he pulled on his jacket and strapped on his motorbike helmet, a sharp, piercing sound interrupted the usual hum of the morning: police whistles.

Instinctively, Brakes tensed and scanned the streets. The whistles seemed to be coming from the south. He quickly mounted his beloved Triumph Speed Twin 5T, a sleek machine in deep burgundy and silver that he had painstakingly kept in pristine condition, despite the war. The roar of its engine drowned out the rest of the world as he twisted the throttle and sped off toward the disturbance.

The streets of Norwich blurred around him as he turned onto Prince of Wales Road, where he spotted a group of uniformed officers running after someone on foot. As Brakes drew closer, he saw their target: a pair of young boys, barely in their teens, riding what appeared to be an American-style army motorcycle, far too large for them. The boy at the back clutched a woman's handbag and a wicker shopping basket—likely the spoils of their latest theft.

"Don't worry boys, I'll get the little bastards!" Brakes yelled over the growling of his engine as he raced past the foot patrol.

Dropping down a gear, he surged ahead in hot pursuit, eyes locked on the fleeing motorcycle. The boys were good—better than most adults he'd encountered—zigzagging through traffic, mounting pavements, and dodging pedestrians without hesitation. The driver was fearless, or perhaps reckless, taking corners at speeds that would terrify any seasoned rider.

The chase was becoming dangerous, pushing both machines and riders to their limits. Brakes considered for a moment whether to back off; it was wartime, and the city could hardly afford casualties from a police chase. But his instincts, sharpened by years on the force, told him these boys wouldn't stop unless forced to.

Turning left, then right, the chase took them down narrower streets, winding through the heart of the city. Both motorcycles weaved in and out of alleyways and side roads. Then, without realising, the boys turned onto a street that had been heavily bombed just days before. The road was littered with rubble, the clean-up only just beginning, and workers were still sifting through the debris in search of survivors. The boys, showing no regard for the devastation around them, sped through the wreckage, sending workers scattering as they rode by.

Brakes knew he had them cornered now. The street was blocked off at the end by a massive pile of rubble, at least six feet high, which the workers had used to close off the road. But the boys showed no signs of slowing down. Instead, they took the obstacle head-on, riding straight up and over the pile of debris like seasoned stuntmen. Brakes hesitated for a moment, slowing his bike slightly as he surveyed the situation. But his stubborn streak kicked in—he wasn't about to let them get away.

Shifting down to third gear, he opened the throttle, unleashing the full power of the 500cc engine. The motorcycle thundered beneath him as he hit the rubble at speed, bouncing violently as the wheels struggled to find traction on the uneven surface. Brakes clung tightly to the handlebars, his body jostling with the impact.

For a brief second, he was airborne, separated from his bike, his heart lodged in his throat as he sailed toward a stationary lorry parked at the bottom of the rubble heap.

The impact was brutal. Brakes' motorbike crashed through the wooden side of the lorry with a deafening crack. Brakes quickly followed, his body a helpless passenger as it smashed through the timber and collided with the hard brick wall of the house behind it. The air in his lungs was violently expunged. Every part of his body reeled in pain as he spiralled to the ground like a lifeless doll. For a moment, everything went silent, the world around him dissolving into a haze of pain and shock.

He tried to move, but his body wouldn't cooperate. His legs felt like they were on fire, and his wrist throbbed with an intensity that made him want to scream. He managed to glance down and saw wood splinters embedded in his legs, blood seeping through his torn trousers. The pain hit him in waves, each one worse than the last, until it was all-consuming.

Voices drifted toward him—people shouting, someone calling for an ambulance. Brakes heard the familiar sound of bells ringing in the distance; the police were approaching, their cars undoubtedly hurtling toward him. He tried to focus, but his vision blurred. One of the first uniformed foot patrol officers on the scene stepped forward, unknowingly crushing his fedora underfoot. *"Why is it that my hat always gets it?"* Brakes thought, managing a weak smile.

"Did anyone see where those boys went?" He croaked, but before anyone could answer, his body finally gave in and the world faded to black.

When Brakes regained consciousness, his surroundings were blurred. He blinked against the harsh overhead light, trying to gather his bearings. A strong smell of disinfectant filled the air. Rubbing his head, he softly stroked over his bumps and flinched. As his vision stabilised, Brakes saw that his arms and legs were heavily bandaged, and his wrist was encased in a thick plaster cast. He didn't feel any pain until a dull throb emanated throughout his whole body, but it was manageable. He attempted to sit up, wincing as every movement sent fresh waves of discomfort through every injury.

The door to his room swung open and in walked the Chief Superintendent, his superior. A man of few words, the Chief was stern and uncompromising, with the hard edge of a former military man who had seen too much of the world's brutality. From his bed, Brakes could see the Chief's handlebar moustache twitch as he surveyed Brakes with a look of disappointment and concern.

"What the bloody hell were you thinking, Brakes?" The Chief barked. "A reckless chase through bombed-out streets? You've put not only yourself but the public at risk!"

Brakes opened his mouth to reply, but the Chief wasn't finished. "You've been riding that blasted motorbike like you're on the front lines! It should never have been used as a police vehicle!"

"I had them, Chief," Brakes said, his voice weak. "I nearly had them."

"*Nearly* doesn't cut it, Inspector," the Chief shot back. "It looks like you've totalled your motorbike, and you're lucky to be alive. As for your disregard for public safety, we'll discuss that in my office once you're released. Your bloodhound mentality is an asset to you and the force, but it is one that will get you killed."

Brakes nodded, though the Chief's words stung. The Chief tossed a bag onto the foot of the bed, Brakes' crushed fedora peeking out from the top. "Someone found your hat," the chief muttered. "Not much good to you now, is it?"

The Chief turned and left without another word, leaving Brakes alone with his thoughts. Reaching for his hat, his face twitched and tightened up as he did so. Laying back, Brakes let out a yelp whilst he placed it gently on the bed beside him. It was a small comfort in the chaos of his life.

The days in the hospital passed slowly. Brakes, unable to do much else, tried to keep himself busy by helping around the ward. He read to other patients, listened to their stories of bombings and accidents, and tried to make light of his own situation. But the war was never far from his mind, the sounds of air raids and bombings filtering through even the thick hospital walls.

By the third day, Brakes had a visitor. His neighbour had brought him some clothes from home and with the help of a nurse, he managed to get dressed. His wounds were healing, though slowly, and the doctors said he could be discharged. They needed the bed for other, more critical cases, after all.

Limping, he stepped out of the hospital. As he clutched his wrist, he felt the familiar weight of the world fall on his shoulders once again. His motorbike was gone, his body ached with every step, and his mind raced with thoughts of the war he wasn't fighting. But the city needed him, and the police station was calling.

As if on cue, a black Wolseley police car pulled up beside him. A young woman in an ATS uniform got out, snapping to attention. "Sir, I'm Vera, your driver. The Chief sent me to collect you."

Brakes raised an eyebrow. "Never call me sir," he said curtly. "It's Brakes, or Inspector if you must. And next time, don't bother opening the door for me. I can manage."

Vera nodded, her cheeks beginning to rouge. "Where to, Inspector?"

"Station," Brakes replied with a tired smile. "I've got an appointment with the Chief."

As they drove through the city, Brakes stared out of the window at the familiar streets of Norwich. The war had left its mark on the city, but life went on. People still shopped, children played in the streets and, despite the devastation, the heart of the city was still beating.

Brakes wasn't sure how long he could tolerate being driven around. He had always made his own way to and from work, but now he had to put up with a driver, and a chatterbox to boot.

"Forgive me for asking," Vera started, her eyes beginning to drift from the road. "But your surname, Brakes, is unusual for these parts. Where does it come from?"

"My parents. They are, in point of fact, American. They came to live here almost thirty years ago, on the south coast," Brakes explained. "Which is where I was born, so, don't worry yourself; I'm British, through and through."

"Well, not to put too finer point on it, but that would make you fifty percent British," Vera unhelpfully supplied.

"I was born here, schooled here, I trained here, my friends are all from here. I'm as British as anyone else born here," Brakes stated with unbreakable certainty.

Suddenly, Vera was braking hard, narrowly missing a horse and cart that came out of nowhere. Unprepared, Brakes was thrust forward, hitting his head on the windscreen and squashing his already broken wrist between him and the dashboard.

"What the fuck!? Are you trying to kill me!" Brakes screamed, spittle flying from his mouth. "You are aware I have recently been in an accident? Are you *trying* to send me back to the hospital?"

"I'm sorry, sir, it just came out of nowhere. Are you okay?" Vera asked, concerned.

"No, no I'm bloody not. Slow down and pay more attention to your duties and less about who I am," he hissed through his teeth, gripping his wrist to dull the thrum of pain coursing through him. "Now, do you think you can get us to the station? In one piece, preferably."

"Yes, sir... Inspector."

Vera continued to drive at less than twenty-five miles per hour, when they arrived at the station without further incident or even a spoken word.

Still clutching his broken wrist, Brakes headed for the Chiefs office. He could feel his forehead beginning to throb from where he had collided with the window—that would leave a nasty bruise in the morning. Two accidents in four days; it was a good job Brakes wasn't the superstitious sort.

Brakes knocked on the Chiefs door and waited for the customary "Enter" to follow, except it never arrived. He knocked again, shouted "Chief," before deciding to finally open the door.

The Chief wasn't there. Allowing himself a sigh of relief, Brakes stepped out of the room and closed the door behind him. He really wasn't looking forward to this encounter.

As Brakes made his way to his own desk, he asked a couple of the permanent station ladies if they knew where the Chief was. They had no idea.

The squad room had six desks in it, all set back-to-back. This had been done so that partners could work in a face-to-face environment. Brakes, however, didn't have a partner; no one would work with him due to his bullish, temerarious methods when out on the field.

Between each set of desks there are large windows framed in a dark oak wood. Everyone else who worked within the area kept their work space clean and tidy. Brakes, however, had needed an extra desk just to keep his filing system on. There was paperwork everywhere; it was a wonder he could make any sense of it at all.

He had only been sat for a few minutes, glancing through the bag snatchers file he was ready to update, when…

"Brakes, if you're in here, get your broken body in my office *RIGHT NOW*!"

Standing from his chair, Brakes made his way back towards the Chiefs office. Glancing around the room, Brakes could see everyone smiling knowingly in his direction. Clearly, news of his most recent efforts had found its way around the office, and fast.

"Sit down, Brakes," the Chief said the moment Brakes stepped into his office. Sitting at his desk, the Chief's gaze hardened while Brakes made his way to the chair across from his superior.

"Now, what am I going to do with you?" The Chief asked, his voice unnervingly even. "You recklessly endanger citizens, not to mention yourself. Ever since you were declined the 'call up', you have gone into self-destruction mode." Standing from his seat, the Chief continued.

"Look, I get it. We all want to be out there fighting for our country, but you need to try and get this straight in your mind: We are vital to the war effort. We keep the home fires burning, the streets safe and speak up for those that no longer can."

The Chief's words were a reminder, one Brakes had heard many times before. That did not make it any less annoying to hear it again, of course.

"I get it, Chief, but that doesn't stop my insides twisting every time I see someone in uniform. I feel disgusted, even ashamed of myself that I am not with them," Brakes explained, trying to keep calm. "I see people pointing. Talking about me. There are others my age that, due to the law passed by parliament, can't join the war effort and are suffering the same kind of disgust from others."

Drawing a deep breath, Brakes shook his head and did his best to quell the simmering emotions that were ready to erupt within him. He heard the Chief sigh, a single finger tapping against the wooden desk.

"It's hard for everyone, Brakes. But you have got to get past this, and I believe I have the just the thing to help you do that." Opening his desk drawer, the Chief pulled out some papers and dropped them in front of Brakes. "There has been a murder. Male, forty-three years of age, amputee. Uniformed officers have closed the scene and are awaiting your arrival at Truston Vicarage."

Picking up the papers, Brakes looked over the information the Chief had given him. While rifling through the files, he heard his superior speak up again, this time from the office window.

"Oh, and Brakes? Remember to be professional." The Chief said, turning his back on the desk. "And no more of your dangerous antics."

CHAPTER TWO

Brakes emerged from the station, bruised and tired, where Vera was already waiting for him. She gave him a tentative smile, still guilty over the accident that had left him with more pain than he cared to acknowledge, and with possible further injury to his wrist. He ignored her. Not in a malicious way, but because he simply couldn't deal with pleasantries right now. Vera started the engine and Brakes hopped into the car. The crime scene loomed ahead—only fifteen miles away—and that distance felt far too short.

The drive was mostly silent, save for Vera's occasional mutterings about how sorry she was for adding to his injuries. Thirty minutes later, they pulled up to the scene. A small crowd had gathered, with the curious onlookers being held back by the local constables. Brakes shot Vera a glance, curt but direct.

"Stay with the car," he ordered and stepped out of the vehicle without waiting for a reply.

The body of John Marsh lay nestled in the tall grass reeds, obscured from the road but not invisible to someone with an attentive dog. Brakes surveyed the area, noting the solitary set of tire tracks leading toward the reeds and back again.

The corpse itself was twisted in an unnatural position, the kind that only happened after severe trauma. Marsh's injuries were vicious—he'd been badly beaten, though that much was obvious even at first glance. There were no signs of multiple comings and goings. The grass was trampled, but only by footprints—no visible drag marks or blood trails leading to the location where the body lay.

It was clear to Brakes that this wasn't where John Marsh had died—it was where he had been dumped.

What struck Brakes immediately, though, was the absence of Marsh's prosthetic leg. The lower half of his right leg was a clean stump, but there was no sign of the prosthetic anywhere nearby. The fact that the limb was missing and there was no signs of struggle at the scene disturbed Brakes. Why take a man's artificial leg?

Brakes scrawled a few quick notes in his pad before heading over to a uniformed officer and the man who had found the body.

"Sir," the officer said, handing over some documents. "The victim's papers. His name was John Marsh. Forty-three years old. Lived at the Marsh Estate, by the River Bure."

"Thanks," Brakes said, barely sparing the papers a glance. He turned to the man who had discovered the body. "Walk me through how you found him."

The man, a local dog walker, fidgeted. "I already told all this to the other officer."

"I need to hear it for myself," Brakes replied evenly. "Please. Start from the beginning."

With a sigh, the man relented. "I walk my dog, Suzi, every morning. We take the same route from my place down toward the sea, past the vicarage, and then on the footpath leading toward St. Mary's Church," he explained, his voice quiet. "I let her off the lead once we're on the path. Everything was normal until Suzi started barking at something in the grass, wouldn't come when I called. I went in after her and… well, that's when I found the body."

"Anything out of the ordinary?" Brakes asked. "Blood? His prosthetic leg?"

"No. No blood. No leg, either," the man answered quickly. "May I go now? Suzi's hungry, and I need to get home."

Brakes nodded. "We'll be in touch if we need anything more."

He gestured toward the paramedics to have the body taken away. The onlookers, still milling about, caught his eye; perhaps they could help search the area. In wartime, it wasn't uncommon to enlist the public's help in such matters.

He instructed the six bystanders, now including Vera, after Brakes beckoned her over to form a line. "Three feet apart," he directed. "If you see anything unusual, stop and shout. We're looking for anything related to the crime, more specifically a prosthetic leg."

They combed through the area systematically, heading up the path toward the vicarage, a handsome red brick building with leaded windows. After circling the building, they returned along the route toward St. Mary's Church. The area was dotted with small lakes and rivers, places that could have easily hidden the body for years. And yet, the killer had chosen to dump Marsh where he would be quickly found. Why? It was a bold, almost careless move.

The questions multiplied. Why take the prosthetic leg? Why beat him so severely and we're still unsure about the ultimate cause of death? Why leave the body where it would be discovered, rather than weigh it down and let it sink in the nearby waters?

They found nothing and, one by one, the onlookers began to disperse. Brakes sighed, knowing that the next step would be even more unpleasant—informing Marsh's family. Vera, however, seemed to be buzzing with excitement. Her first real case was proving to be far more than she had ever anticipated.

"Let's go," Brakes sighed. It would be better to get the process of announcing Marsh's death over and done with. With Vera following close behind, Brakes made his way back to the car.

Fifteen miles later, they pulled up at the Marsh Estate, a sprawling property on the banks of the River Bure. A large sandstone mansion loomed over the land. Stepping out of the car, Brakes instructed Vera to stay in the vehicle again and approached the front door. He knocked; the weight of the metal knocker heavy on the door as it echoed throughout the quiet estate grounds. A moment later the door opened to reveal a housemaid, just barely out of her teens.

"Inspector Brakes, Norwich Police," he said by way of introduction. "I need to speak to the lady or gentleman of the house."

Nodding, the maid led him through a grand hallway to a back parlour with wide windows overlooking the serene river. Positioning himself by the window, Brakes allowed the calming view to settle his thoughts until a soft voice interrupted him.

"Inspector Brakes?"

He turned to see a striking woman in her late twenties, with jet-black hair and piercing blue eyes that were almost unnaturally bright against her pale skin. She smiled politely, though her eyes reflected concern.

"I am Ann Marsh. Rosie—that is, my housemaid— said you wished to see me. What's this about?" Ann asked whilst gesturing to Brakes to be seated opposite her.

Brakes cleared his throat, taking a seat on the sofa across from her. "I need to ask you about your brother, John."

Ann's smile faltered. "What has he done now?" She asked with a faint laugh. "He's always getting into some sort of trouble. Ever since the accident, he's been... difficult."

"Accident?"

Ann nodded, her expression softening. "Our parents died in a car crash several years ago. John lost his leg in the same accident. I think he blames himself for it, though he'd never admit that to anyone."

Brakes made a mental note of that. "I'm sorry for your loss, Miss Marsh. May I call you Ann?"

"Of course," she replied.

"There's no easy way to say this," Brakes began, choosing his words carefully. "John's body was found this morning near Truston Vicarage."

The words seemed to knock the breath from her body. Ann's face drained of colour as she stared at him, her composure crumbling. At that moment, the housemaid, Rosie, entered the room carrying a tea tray. Looking at Ann's face, which now held a blank, cold stillness, Rosie placed the tray on the table between the sofa's and hastily went to stand by her side.

"Ann! What's wrong?" She asked, kneeling beside Ann and taking hold of her hand.

Brakes found the gesture unusually intimate for a housemaid, but he let it pass. Ann stammered something incoherent, her body trembling as she tried to fight back the tears. Brakes felt an odd pang of sympathy for the young woman.

"Is there anyone we can call for you?" He asked softly.

Ann shook her head, her voice barely audible. "No… no. I'm all that's left. I have no family now."

With a final choked sob, she fled the room, leaving Brakes with Rosie. The maid glanced at him, her eyes equally blue and just as piercing. They were close in age, and for a moment, Brakes couldn't help but notice a strange resemblance between the two women.

Then, after a long pause, Brakes said, "Please, show me to John's room."

Rosie stood silently for a moment, as though deciding whether to refuse, before nodding and leading him upstairs. The house was grand but not lavish, its hallways quiet except for the sound of Rosie and Brakes' footsteps echoing against the floorboards.

"How did he die?" Rosie asked as they climbed the staircase.

"We're still figuring that out," Brakes replied, dodging the full truth for now. "You and Miss Marsh seem quite close."

Rosie smiled faintly. "We grew up together. My mother worked here as the housemaid for over thirty years. When she passed, Ann asked me to stay on. We've always been close; more like sisters than employer and maid."

"And your father? Is he still with us?"

"No. Sadly, he died from his injuries during the first war many years ago. Mother never re-married."

The pieces began to click into place for Brakes. Sisters, or something more complicated than that?

They reached John's room, which was sparsely furnished. A bed, a wardrobe, a chest of drawers and nothing more. It didn't take long for Brakes to find what he was looking for—or rather, what he wasn't. John's prosthetic leg was tucked inside the wardrobe.

"Is this the missing leg? from the crime scene?" Brakes wondered to himself whilst picking it up.

"Curious," Brakes muttered to himself. If John had left the house without his prosthetic, where were his crutches? They were not at the crime scene, either. Rosie soon left John's room, and Brakes was grateful for the privacy.

After a thorough search yielded nothing else of interest, Brakes made his way back downstairs. Ann had returned to the parlour, her face streaked with tear marks but otherwise composed.

"I'm sorry to press you in your grief, Ann, but I need to know more about your brother's life. Did he ever leave the house without his prosthetic leg?" Brakes asked.

Ann shook her head. "Never. He was too self-conscious about it. He hated being seen with crutches. Why?"

"I found his artificial leg in his wardrobe," Brakes replied.

"Oh, no. No, no, that's his second one," Ann said quickly with a shake of her head. "He had a replacement made years ago, just in case he needed it."

"Are they both made the same?" Brakes asked. "By the same company?"

"Yes, metal and leather, lightweight," she explained. "Are you saying it is missing? Why would they take his leg? It has no value."

"I am trying to figure that out, Ann," Brakes said, his voice gentle so as not to upset her further. "I may need to visit you again in the future. The coroner will let you know when your brother's body will be available for collection. Thank you for your time."

Turning, Brakes made his way towards the door to leave. Ann simply stood there, silent, her eyes rimmed red as she stared out of the window.

Brakes hesitated for a moment, then turned to ask, "Was there anyone he might have had a dispute with? Anyone who would want to harm him?"

Ann's eyes widened, and she looked away. "Not that I know of," she said, but her voice wavered. "John had... issues, but he wasn't violent. Just... troubled."

Brakes leaned forward, catching her eye. "I need to know everything, Ann. If there's something you're not telling me, now is the time."

"No," Ann whispered, shaking her head as she tried to hold back her tears. "I have nothing more to add, Inspector."

Brakes hesitated. He had a gut feeling that Ann was holding back, but in a bid to allow her time to grieve, he gave a final nod and made his exit. As the door closed heavily behind him, he paused for a few seconds on the front door step, mulling over all that had transpired. Finally, he returned to the car.

"Home please, Vera," Brakes sighed, sliding into the passenger seat. "They are bringing what is left of my motorcycle home and I want to be there when they arrive."

Brakes had been home a little over an hour when there was a knock at the door. It was the men delivering his motorbike. Tiredly, he requested that they put what was left of the vehicle in his garage. Once they had left, Brakes took the time to finally take a look at what had become of his beloved motorbike.

The whole front end had become a tangled mess of metal and wires. The petrol tank had a big dent in it, and one of the exhausts had been ripped off completely. It was clear that, while restoring his beloved motorbike was possible, it would have to wait until Brakes' wrist had healed. For now, all he could do was throw a sheet over it and close the garage doors.

Returning to the house, Brakes went to pour himself a stiff drink, only to find that he had run out. Though he was not an excessive drinker, he did like to keep a bottle of Scotch on hand, especially for occasions such as this.

Feeling even more deflated, Brakes put the Scotch bottle down with a sigh. Grabbing his coat, he decided on a visit to his close friend, Doug.

His friend since childhood, Brakes and Doug had become closer in more recent years due to their shared mental anguish over not being able to join their other mates on the front line. Now a flight training officer, Doug worked at RAF Mousehold Heath where British, American and even Polish pilots were trained.

The distinctive, yellow-coloured training aircraft that was housed there—a Miles M.14 Magister—was a regular sight in the skies above the city. Similarly, the streets of Norwich were regularly populated with various uniformed officers, both men and women, all from the America's, Poland and Britain.

The American's hadn't officially joined the war yet. However, many US citizens had felt the need to volunteer, with many of them already having family living in Britain. Others simply wanted to join the struggle or had followed their friends over.

As in most towns and cities around the country, the black-market scene was a major blight on all concerned. Doug didn't partake in any kind of black-market goods; however, he did have a solid supply of whisky and other US goods through gifts from the graduating pilots he had trained. Brakes could usually find Doug at the Bell Hotel, which doubled as a dormitory for the American Women's Army Air Corps on the top floor.

The Bell was situated on Oxford Hill, not too far from the marketplace. This location was, in fact, one of a few reasons why Brakes enjoyed taking his morning tea in the marketplace. It allowed him to engage in a ritual of morning greetings with many uniformed women as they walked through the market to work.

There was no denying that Doug enjoyed being surrounded by beautiful ladies in uniform, too; it was predominantly why the Bell Hotel had become one of his friend's favourite spots to spend his time.

Brakes walked into the Bell and searched the bar for Doug. Though it had just opened for the day, the bar was already quite busy with a mixture of regular patrons and uniformed officers. Almost everywhere he looked, Brakes could see that every dark oak table had been taken. The beer, mild and bitter, was clearly going down well; he could already spy a collection of empty glasses growing on various tables.

Making his way through the sea of blue, brown and a couple of black uniforms. Scanning the room once more, Brakes finally spotted Doug sat on a table in the corner, close to the piano. Waving to catch his attention, Brakes gestured to his friend to see if he needed another pint. Catching Brakes' eye, Doug lifted his pint glass and gave a thumbs up.

Even though there were two people working the bar, it took several minutes for Brakes to finally get served. Once he had his drinks though, he realised he had a problem: How would he carry two pints of beer with a broken wrist?

Logically, taking two trips would be the best course of action, but with the ever-increasing crowd, it would be a slow process. Sighing, Brakes left his pint on the bar and, taking Doug's pint, made his way through the crowd to his friends' table.

"You sit down, mate," Doug said quickly, clearly having seen Brakes' struggle. "I'll grab your pint."

Doug left for the bar while Brakes took a seat. His friend was quick to return to the table with the second drink and settled back down.

"You didn't bother to visit me in hospital, then?" Brakes asked, his question not at all malicious. Doug simply smiled and took a glug of his pint.

"I knew you weren't going to die; how many times have you come off that bloody thing anyway? At least twelve times now, right?" Doug chuckled and shook his head. "Yes, you always break something, but you always seem to walk out under your own steam. So, no, I didn't see any point in visiting. I knew you'd find me afterwards, anyway."

"Well, I love your confidence in my ability to outdo my self-destructive nature," Brakes grinned, and lifted his pint glass with his good hand. "To celebrate, what's the chances of a bottle of your finest Scotch, then?"

"I knew it," Doug said, laughter escaping him. "And I'm well ahead of you, Brakes. Here ya go." A second later, Doug was producing a bottle from his coat pocket and handed it over to Brakes. "Now, you go easy with that—we don't want you falling over and breaking anything else, now, do we?"

CHAPTER THREE

Brakes awoke early the next morning and spent an hour in the garage. Using only his good hand, he started the grim task of stripping down his bike. Once Vera arrived, Brakes cleaned up and allowed her to help him change some of his bandages.

His injuries seemed to be healing well. Once Vera had finished, they set off to visit the medical officer in the hope that he had completed his examination on John's remains. Of course, Brakes was also eager to know if the man could possibly provide further information to aid him in solving the murder.

Upon his arrival, Brakes was greeted with a putrid odour—one reminiscent of rotting meat—as well as the sight of Marsh's bruise-mottled body lying on the table before him. Hunched over him was the medical officer, a stern man Brakes had known for a good few years, now.

"Ah, Brakes, good timing; I have a few things here that you will find interesting," the medical officer said, looking up from the table the moment Brakes entered the room.

"Really?" Brakes asked, closing the door behind him. "You have something that will shed some light on this?"

"Well, more muddy waters than clear, bright skies," the medical officer replied with a grim chuckle. "Firstly, he didn't die from a beating. Although his injuries were quite severe, if the man had sought medical attention, he may well have lived. No, he was drowned."

Brakes nodded. He had known as much from his own findings, though he did not need to reiterate this with the medical officer. Turning back to his findings, the medical officers focus drifted away from Brakes.

"Not in sea water, but fresh water," the man continued, his voice growing to a mumble. "Not very clean fresh water, either; from a river, perhaps." Looking up again, the medical officer's gaze returned to Brakes. "Secondly, there were these—I found them in his sock. Two different pieces of envelope, both from the seal part. Sweetheart letters, I believe."

The medical officer proceeded to hold up two indistinct scraps of paper, wrinkled from water damage. Blinking, Brakes stepped closer to get a better look.

"What makes you say that?" He asked, carefully taking them from the medical officer.

"The acronyms written on them," he replied, pointing to the lettering on the envelope scraps. "As you can see, '*I.T.A.L.Y.*' and '*S.W.A.K.*' have been added here and, judging by the handwriting, was written by the same person."

Returning to the body, the medical officer indicated a gloved hand to the body's chest. Shuffling closer to the table, Brakes could clearly see two small, brown marks, perhaps formed during Marsh's beating.

"Then there are these two small puncture wounds on his chest," the medical officer continued with a frown. "Not life threatening, nor were they made by the blade of a knife. They are quite small in diameter, twelve inches apart to be exact, and there is rust both in and around the wounds."

Brakes remained quiet, his thoughts beginning to spiral. Rust in the wounds? Whatever could that mean? The medical officer looked up at Brakes again, his gaze becoming quite serious.

"If I had to guess, Brakes, then I would say that these wounds were made by small, rusty nails," the medical officer offered, his tone final.

Brakes stared down at the body, his lips twisting into a frown. The case was becoming far more curious, it seemed. It was clear Marsh had been murdered, not by beating but by drowning. Now, he was carrying two pieces of different envelopes with acronyms in his sock. And whatever could be the purpose of those two nail holes in his chest?

Sighing, Brakes turned to the medical officer and offered him a nod. "Thank you," he said, already feeling tired from the events of the day. "I believe that will be all for today. I shall be on my way." And with a tip of his hat, Brakes left the facility.

Once he had returned to the car, Brakes requested for Vera to take him back to the Marsh estate. As they drove, a few more questions swirled in his mind.

Why hadn't Ann Marsh informed him that John Marsh had been walking out with someone, and why hadn't he found any letters in his bedroom when he searched it last time?

"You seem quite puzzled, sir," Vera asked, driving in the direction of the estate.

Exasperated, Brakes scrubbed a hand over his face. "Vera, you're here to drive me—you are not here to get involved in anything else," he replied tersely. "But since you ask, yes. This case seems to be coming up with more questions than answers."

Brakes proceeded to hold up the two slithers of envelope that had been found in John's sock. Vera gave them both a discerning glance, but only briefly, before turning her eyes back to the road. It seemed like she had learned her lesson from before.

"I apologise, sir. It's just that this is my first murder, and honestly, it has sparked a deep interest within me," she explained, before falling into silence. Slipping the evidence back into his pocket, Brakes felt quite thankful for the quiet as the world passed them by.

It only took a few minutes before Vera broke the silence again. It was becoming clear to Brakes that, when it came to Vera, listening wasn't one of her strong points.

"Sir," she began, almost tentatively. "The pieces of paper you have. They are from sweetheart letters, aren't they?"

At this question, Brakes audibly groaned. "Vera, we have spoken about this," he snapped, his ire at her second disturbance a clear warning. Vera, of course, ignored it.

"Sorry, sir," she continued, not sounding sorry at all. "It's just that the handwriting looks quite manly, I think. Clearly, they were in a strong relationship, the acronym 'S.W.A.K' (*Sealed With A Kiss*) clearly shows that." Vera replied, veering over to the opposite oncoming lane.

"For god's sake, Vera! Eyes on the road!" Brakes snapped.

She fell silent again as Brakes, slightly taken aback, quickly pulled the slips of envelope from his pocket again. Taking a closer look, he could see that Vera was right—the lettering looked quite masculine as opposed to the slightly curved, more feminine look a woman's penmanship might hold.

"*Well, I'll be,*" Brakes thought as he studied each slip of paper. "*Vera, although totally frustrating most of the time, might actually be onto something.*"

Upon arriving at the estate, Brakes headed for the front door and rang the bell. Rosie answered the door again and, without much need for greeting, immediately led Brakes to the rear of the property. There, Ann was sitting in the garden alone taking tea. Despite the current circumstances, she seemed eerily at ease. Where most young women would be beside themselves with grief, Ann seemed as if she had hardly cried since the first time Brakes had met her. Ann might be shocked, Brakes reminded himself, however her body language did not lend any weight to that theory.

Without further instruction, Rosie quickly left so that Brakes could talk with Ann privately.

"Good morning," Brakes called, breaking Ann from her reverie. "Sorry to bother you again so soon, Ann."

"Inspector," Ann returned, taking a sip of her tea. "How may I help you today?"

Brakes wasn't here for pleasantries, deciding instead to get straight to the point. Taking a seat at the table across from her, Brakes shot Ann a pointed look.

"It seems you have not been entirely honest with me since our last meeting, now, have you?" He said almost scathingly. At this, Ann's eyebrows shot up as she set her teacup down.

"Whatever do you mean?" She asked, understandably perplexed by Brakes' accusation.

"Well, for a start you never told me that John had a sweetheart," Brakes claimed all too bitterly, and pulled the two pieces of envelope from his pocket to place them on the table. "Now, would you mind telling me exactly who she is?"

He watched closely as Ann surveyed the evidence, understanding slowly dawning on her features.

"Inspector, these are from my letters," she said, her voice slower than normal. "Not John's. Whatever was he doing with them?"

She looked up at him, her blue eyes wide and filled with concern and far more questions than Brakes cared to answer. In that moment he wished he hadn't been so quick to accuse Ann of dishonesty. Clearing his throat, Brakes chose to quickly answer her question.

"They were found in his sock. A curious place to hide them, don't you think?" He explained. Ann nodded and took another sip of tea. "And if they are yours, then why would John feel the need to remove these two pieces from the envelopes?"

Ann was quiet, as if pondering this question herself. Brakes allowed her a moment with her thoughts before finally asking, "Where are the letters, Ann? Could you get them for me, please?"

Without hesitation, Ann gave Brakes a stiff nod and stood from her seat. Heading towards the house, she entered through the patio doors and immediately called for Rosie to collect the letters from her room and to bring them to her.

A few minutes later, Rosie arrived with a bundle of about fifteen letters tied together with twine. Setting them on the table, she left again while Brakes set to work. While Ann took her seat again and sipped her cooling tea, Brakes took his time perusing through the letters.

They dated back to over two years, all of them signed with the initial 'B.' The postmarks were the most interesting aspect, with all of them sent from different countries. It was clear this man was very well travelled.

"Who is 'B,' and what does he do for a living?" Brakes enquired.

"His name is Brian," Ann replied, finishing off her tea. "He's a third-generation food manufacturer with factories in several countries."

Brakes nodded and looked through the letters again. Although they contained the usual sentiments of a normal sweetheart letter—talk of missing a loved one, a promise to meet again—there also seemed to be something lacking in each one. What that was, however, Brakes couldn't be certain.

Eventually, Brakes found the two letters from the missing envelope seals. Much like the others, they appeared to be normal love letters. So, it begged the question: Why had John removed the seals and placed them in his sock?

When he asked Ann this very question once more, she simply shook her head while sipping on her tea.

"I honestly couldn't say, Inspector," she replied with a sigh.

It seemed Ann had fewer answers than Brakes had anticipated. Placing the evidence back into his pocket, Brakes decided to instead focus on something that might garner some results.

"Did John have a girl in his life?" He asked. At this Ann nodded and, almost nervously, busied herself with putting the letters back in order.

"Yes. Several over the years, in fact, though there hasn't been anyone recently, I believe," Ann confirmed. "I do, however, know that the last two girls he stepped out with worked at the Gardeners Arms."

Brakes nodded. This was the lead he needed. Standing, he looked down at the letters, once again bundled and tied together with twine, and asked,

"May I take the letters with me? To help aid in the investigation."

"Of course, Inspector," Ann replied, her smile slight. "Anything to help find my brother's killer."

Brakes took the letters from the table. He would look into them further at the station. For now, though, he had more pressing matters to attend to.

"Thank you," he murmured, offering the young woman a stiff nod. "For now, I suggest that you do not leave the area; I may well have further questions at a later date. Good day, Ann." And with a final tip of his hat, Brakes turned on his heel and left the estate.

Returning to the car, he instructed Vera to take him to the Gardeners Arms or, as Brakes knew it, the 'Murderers Arms.' Upon hearing the pub's nickname, Vera visibly perked up as she started the drive into the city centre.

"Do you know why it's called that?" She asked, seeming genuine in her curiosity as she turned a corner. Brakes nodded.

"Yes, I do," he replied. "Back in the late 1800s, a man beat his wife to death in the bar. That's how the name came to be."

At this, Vera smiled widely. "This is awesome," she exclaims, practically bouncing in her seat. "My first murder, and now we're going to the 'Murderers Arms.' This is so exciting."

Vera parked on Timber Street, not far from The Bell Hotel. Getting out of the car, she began what Brakes considered to be her usual routine—a walk around the car to do some checks on the vehicle, before taking out a rag for cleaning the windows. It was a means to help Vera to pass time while Brakes was working, though he did wonder if she found it incredibly dull.

Brakes, however, stayed in the car. He sat motionless, his gaze wandering into the distance while barely managing to focus on anything. Finally, after an uncertain amount of time, he heard a knock on the window. Blinking, he turned to find Vera watching him, a frown on her lips.

"Sir, are you okay?" She asked. Silently, Brakes gave her a nod before swinging the door open, almost knocking Vera back. Stumbling, she managed to catch herself in time.

"I might be a while," Brakes muttered, slamming the door shut behind him. "Go grab a cup of tea or something."

Vera glanced up the street towards the hotel. With a nod, she began walking towards the Bell. It was a cosy spot, boasting not only a fine cup of tea, but an impressive view of the ancient castle that loomed proudly over its city.

The mediaeval fortress—more recently equipped with anti-aircraft guns and searchlights—felt as imposing as ever. Brakes had often wondered what the castle must have looked like to invaders centuries ago, as even now it sent a clear message of strength and dominance to all who looked upon it.

Making his way to the pub, Brakes caught sight of the landlord and a woman scrubbing the front windows. Dust from the most recent bombings still clung to everything, and for many business owners in the area, cleaning had become an everyday task.

The landlord was a burly man. His nose, once tall, looked as if it had been crushed beneath more than a hundred fists. His neck alone was almost the size of Brakes' legs, while his thick arms looked like they were capable of doing some damage. It would not have surprised Brakes to learn that this man had once found his calling in the middle of a boxing ring.

The woman beside him seemed younger, perhaps in her late twenties or early thirties if Brakes were to guess. With honey-blonde hair pinned back into fashionable curls, it was quite obvious to anyone that looked her way that she was an attractive lass. Perhaps she had been one of the young ladies John Marsh had taken an interest in?

It was the woman that noticed Brakes first, her dark eyes narrowing with suspicion.

"Heads up," she snapped, dunking her rag into the bucket near her feet. "Copper." Jerking her head, she signalled Brakes' presence to her companion. The landlord turned; his own gaze grew wary while the woman dragged her rag back out of the water to continue cleaning.

"Good morning," Brakes called, approaching them with a flash of his identification. "DI Brakes. Could I have a moment of your time?"

The landlord wiped his hands on his apron, watching Brakes closely with a hint of curiosity. "If this is about the scrap last night, no one got hurt," he said, his voice gruff. "I tossed 'em out before it got too bad."

Brakes shook his head. "This isn't about a fight. It's about a murder," he explained, his gaze level with the landlord's. "I need to speak to the woman who was seeing a Mr. John Marsh."

The landlord paused, and his face darkened. Without a word, he nodded toward the woman cleaning the windows. She turned toward Brakes and threw her rag back into the bucket. Water sloshed over the sides while she wiped her hands on her skirt.

"Who's he gone and killed then?" She asked sharply, placing her hands on her hips. "Always knew that man was a rummen."

"What do you mean by that?" Asked Brakes as he took a step closer to the woman.

"We weren't together long. Barely a month," she explained, her mouth twisting into a frown. "He was... off, you know? Like he relived losing his leg every day. Always angry, especially when he'd had a drink." She gestured for Brakes to sit on a nearby bench while he noted the tension in her voice.

"Did he ever get violent with you?" He asked, taking the offered seat. The woman seemed shocked by Brakes' question.

"Violent? Nah, not with me. Barely even touched me. But he was in his own world, always picking fights. He got thrown out of here more times than I can count."

Almost like clockwork, the landlord called from the doorway, "Don't keep her long! We've got a bloody pub to open, ya know!"

Brakes nodded in acknowledgement before turning back to the woman. "He was seeing another woman here too, wasn't he?"

The woman shrugged. "Yeah, Jenny Marsden. But that didn't last long. Not even a week. Not long after they broke up, she moved back to her parents, in Peterborough." She paused, staring off into the distance before adding "He was generous, well-dressed, lived in a big house—seemed like a catch. But once you got to know him..." She trailed off, shaking her head. "Who's he killed?"

Brakes hesitated. "No one. He's the victim."

Her eyes widened as realisation dawned on her, and for a moment, she seemed genuinely shocked.

"A rummen to the core, but he didn't deserve that," she said, her voice smaller than before. "You should be looking at his sister. Something's not right with her, either. Strange woman, came around here twice, but never stayed long. She gave me the creeps."

She turned abruptly and headed back inside the pub, leaving Brakes to mull over her words. He jotted down the name of the other woman—Jenny Marsden, from Peterborough—and sat in silence for a few minutes, absorbing the information.

Deciding he needed to clear his head, Brakes wandered down Orford Hill, turning right onto Red Lion Street. His walk was more of a slow, contemplative stroll, punctuated by frequent stops. At one point he even removed his hat to run a hand through his hair in frustration.

The distant sound of police whistles interrupted his thoughts. Before he could react, two boys on an army motorcycle came roaring down the street toward him. Instinctively, Brakes raised his hand to signal them to stop, but they just laughed and, as they zoomed past, the boy on the back reached out and knocked Brakes' hat clean off his head.

He watched as they sped away, his blood beginning to simmer. Brakes knew those boys considered it a game; they would more than likely steal someone's shopping for the thrill of the chase. There was a war going on, though, and petty theft during a time of struggle was no laughing matter.

He bent down, retrieved his hat, and brushed it off, muttering to himself, "Always my hat, the little bastards." As he lifted his hat to his head, Brakes paused. With the incident between him and the boys still clear in his mind, Brakes wondered if something similar might have happened days prior—perhaps a possible motive for John Marsh's death.

Could it have been a bar fight gone wrong? Had someone mocked his prosthetic leg until things escalated and it was too late? The theory made sense, but there were still too many gaps.

First of all, where was Marsh's false leg? Why take it? What could have caused those strange holes in his chest? And there was still the issue of why two pieces of envelope had been found in his sock.

Brakes then thought back to Ann. How eerily calm and collected she seemed even a day after the devastating news of her brother's death. How she had withheld the knowledge of her brother having a sweetheart until asked and seemed to have a habit of holding back information even when pressed. And now the comments on Ann's persona from the barmaid?

It felt all too strange, and Brakes had a sure feeling that Ann knew something about John Marsh's murder.

Brakes' thoughts were interrupted as he approached The Bell Hotel again. Vera was sitting outside, sipping her tea, the castle dominating the skyline behind her. He sat down with a heavy sigh, accepting the cup of tea she offered.

"Looks like the best thing that's going to happen today," he muttered, taking a long sip.

Vera raised an eyebrow. "Things not going well, sir?"

Brakes shook his head. "We need to go back to the Marsh estate. Finish your tea; we've got work to do."

After a quiet drive, they arrived at the Marsh estate, which seemed unusually lively. Several cars were parked in the driveway, and voices could be heard coming from the back of the house.

"Seems like she's got company, sir," Vera remarked.

"Indeed," Brakes replied, stepping out of the car. "Come with me. I may need your help."

They followed the sounds of voices to the sunroom at the rear of the house. Inside, they found about fifteen well-dressed women, all amiably chatting away. Brakes scanned the room, his sharp, determined gaze spotting Ann Marsh among a small crowd. He nudged Vera and nodded for her to follow him.

"Ann Marsh," Brakes called, his voice cutting through the chatter like a knife. The room fell silent. "I'm arresting you on suspicion of murdering your brother, John Marsh."

When Vera stepped forward with a pair of handcuffs, Ann's face paled. All eyes in the room turned to her. "What? You can't be serious! Why would I want to kill him?" She protested, but did not resist as Brakes cuffed her.

The other women began to loudly object, but Brakes ignored them. As he marched Ann out to the car, they were followed by a cacophony of voices. One woman even tried to block the door, but a sharp look from Brakes sent her scurrying back.

In the car, Ann loudly insisted on her innocence all the way to the station. Brakes sat quietly and glanced at Vera, who had a small, satisfied smile on her face. But even though Vera stayed quiet, the journey seemed longer than it was with Ann's relentless complaints filling the air.

At the station, the desk sergeant began booking Ann in, but the process was slowed by her incessant protests. As if things couldn't get worse, the front doors flew open, and the women from Ann's tea party stormed into the station, their arms and mouths flailing like a gaggle of angry geese, creating a scene of chaos. Their shouting made it impossible to hear anything clearly.

Suddenly, the shrill blast of a police whistle pierced the air. The gaggle of women immediately quieted, and everyone turned; the Chief had arrived, his neck and face a dangerous red as his presence began to restore order to the station.

"Get this crowd under control!" he bellowed, glaring at every face present in the room. "Or I'll have them all arrested!"

Uniformed officers scrambled to usher the women outside. The Chief stormed back to his office upstairs with Brakes following a safe distance behind. Once they had both entered the room, the Chief slammed the door behind Brakes.

"What in God's name is this, Brakes?" The Chief roared, his face beginning to turn purple. "You've turned the station into a circus!"

Brakes stood his ground. "Sir, I've arrested Ann Marsh on suspicion of murder. She's hiding something, and I thought it best to bring her in," he explained carefully. "It is not my fault her gaggle of friends followed us to the station."

The Chief narrowed his eyes. "Do you have evidence?"

Brakes hesitated. "Not yet. It's a scare tactic; I need to get her to open up." He admitted. "She's withholding vital information, I'm sure of it."

The Chief sighed, rubbing his temples. "Fine. Conduct your interview. But I want a full report afterward, and you'd better not be wasting my time."

Brakes nodded and left to prepare for the interview. Ann was hiding something—he just had to get it out of her.

CHAPTER FOUR

Ann Marsh Interview

Brakes shuffled the papers in the Marsh file. Tapping them on one edge to straighten them, he stood up from his desk and headed towards the interview room with Vera hot on his heels. With one hand on the door handle he turned to Vera.

"And where do you think you're going, Vera?" He asked.

"I thought I might sit in and maybe learn some interview techniques, sir," she said, inching closer to Brakes.

"Vera, must I have to remind you that you're not a police officer? You're my driver. Now, go and wash the car or make some tea."

At his words, Vera's jaw dropped, and the excitement drained from her face with the pace of a speeding car.

Stepping into the dimly lit interrogation room, Brakes saw Ann Marsh pace back and forth, shaking her head and muttering to herself. A female constable stood by the door.

"Sit down, Miss Marsh," Brakes instructed calmly. "This is your last chance to tell me everything."

Ann's eyes flashed with defiance. "I didn't kill my brother!"

Brakes leaned forward, his palms braced against the table. "But you're hiding something. And if you don't come clean, it's going to be a lot worse for you."

Ann hesitated, then finally sat down, folding her arms across her chest. "John was… involved in something. I don't know what. But I know it was dangerous."

Brakes took a seat across from her and raised an eyebrow. "Dangerous how?"

"I don't know. He wouldn't tell me. He just… changed." Ann shook her head and took a shuddering breath. "He became secretive. Paranoid. Always locking himself away in his study. I think he was being blackmailed, but I don't know by whom."

Brakes' heart raced. This was what he'd been waiting for. Now, he just had to dig deeper.

"What makes you think he was being blackmailed?" He asked, managing to keep his voice calm but firm.

"It was the letters. He'd get these envelopes, all marked urgent," Ann explained, biting her lip. Brakes noted that she had started wringing her hands in her lap. "He'd open them in his study, then burn them straight away. I saw him do it more than once. And there were phone calls too—late at night. He'd shut the door and lower his voice so I couldn't hear."

"Did you ever manage to read any of the letters?" Brakes asked. Ann shook her head.

"No. He kept them hidden or destroyed them immediately. The last one came just two days before he was killed." Ann's body shook as she took a deep breath. "I remember because he was in a foul mood after that. More anxious than usual, and he drank heavily that night."

Brakes leaned further into the table, his gaze penetrating while Ann continued to fidget in her seat. "Do you know who sent the letters? Anything about where they came from?" He asked, trying to keep the momentum going.

Ann hesitated, then shook her head again. "I don't. But once, when I went into the study to clean, I saw a name scrawled on the edge of a torn envelope he hadn't quite managed to burn. 'JM,' it said."

JM. John Marsh? The initials matched. "And you're sure it wasn't addressed to him?" Brakes asked.

Ann nodded. "I'm positive. His name was never on those envelopes. He always received them through intermediaries," she explained slowly. "They were sometimes left for him at the post office, other times brought by men I'd never seen before. They'd drop it off and leave without a word."

Brakes made a quick note. Whoever was behind the letters had to be part of a bigger network. This wasn't just a personal vendetta—it was something more organised, more dangerous. Brakes sat in the opposite chair. "Did your brother ever mention anyone named 'JM'?"

Ann shook her head. "No, never." She paused for a moment, then added, "His letters... the intermediaries always marked them with their initials, so that John knew who they were from."

"What about the night of his death?" Brakes pressed her. "Do you remember anything unusual? Did he say or do anything out of the ordinary?"

She closed her eyes as if trying to recount the memory. "He was out late, like most nights, but that evening he came home earlier than usual. I heard him pacing in his room, muttering to himself." Ann paused for a moment, blinked up at the ceiling and swallowed. Returning her gaze to Brakes, she continued. "Then he locked himself in the study. I didn't see or hear from him again until the next morning, when you came to tell me you had found him."

Her voice wavered on the last few words, and Brakes could tell she was close to breaking down, her body seemingly trembling under the pressure. Brakes pressed on, there was more he needed to know.

"Did you hear anything that night? Anything suspicious—footsteps, voices, anything?"

Ann hesitated again, worrying her bottom lip even harder between her teeth. If she wasn't careful, Brakes feared she might draw blood.

"I heard him arguing with someone over the phone earlier that evening. It was about money, I think." She swallowed. Her voice had started to shake. "He was shouting, demanding that they stop, saying something about 'debt' and 'ruining everything.' I've never heard him so desperate."

Brakes nodded, jotting down a few more notes as Ann spoke. Looking up, Brakes asks, "And you don't know who he was speaking to?"

Ann shook her head again. "No. He hung up before I could make out any names."

Brakes ran his hand through his hair, trying to piece together the puzzle. John Marsh was most likely being blackmailed. Someone was squeezing him, threatening him, maybe for debts or secrets he couldn't afford to let slip. And on the night of his death, they'd reached a breaking point.

Brakes stood and began pacing the room, his finger poised on his chin. "The letters, the phone calls, the desperation—it all points to something bigger. From what I have found out so far, your bother wasn't the type of man to back down from anyone, man like your brother doesn't crumble over small matters. This is serious."

Ann watched as Brakes circled the table, mumbling to himself. Her eyes grew with fear. "Do you think whoever might have been blackmailing him killed him?"

Brakes turned to her. "It's a strong possibility, but we need more." Bracing his hands against the table again, Brakes leaned in towards Ann. "You said earlier your brother locked himself away in his study. Did he keep anything in there—papers, documents, anything that could help us?"

Ann hesitated, nervously glancing at the female constable. then back at Brakes. "He kept a safe in the study. I don't know the combination, but he always said that everything important was in there. It's hidden behind a large painting. But I'm sure it's locked."

Brakes paused for a moment.

"Can you show me where it is?" He asked. Ann blinked, exhaustion finally settling into every crevice of her face. Slowly, she nodded, a weary sigh escaping her lips.

"Yes," she murmured, her voice small. "Yes. I can show you."

And with as much strength as she could muster, Ann pushed her chair back and made her way out of the room. Brakes pushed open the door for her and promptly followed her out. Exiting the station, they found Vera waiting for them at the car.

CHAPTER FIVE

They arrived at the Marsh estate an hour later. The house felt eerily quiet as Ann led them through the dimly lit hallways, her footsteps soft on the hardwood floors. Brakes and Vera followed close behind, both alert for any sign that something was out of place.

The study was a large, oak-panelled room with tall windows that overlooked the garden. A heavy wooden desk dominated the centre of the room, covered in papers and half-filled glasses of whisky. Brakes immediately noticed the faint smell of burnt paper that lingered in the air, confirming Ann's story about the destroyed letters.

"There," Ann whispers, pointing to a corner of the room. Brakes stared, dumbfounded; she was pointing at a large oil painting, framed in an antique gold. Then, as if to answer his question, Ann moved towards it and, with all the strength she could muster, pulled the painting off the wall.

There, built into the wall and concealed behind the painting, was a large metal safe. Vera moved to inspect it.

"This is no small-time lock. We'll need a professional to open this, sir," she explained, still looking over the safe. Brakes raised an eyebrow.

"And just how would you know that, Vera?" He asked tersely, walking over to the safe to take a closer look.

"Well, sir, it's like this; my family are in safe's," Vera replied, finally looking up at Brakes.

"Excuse me? What on earth do you mean?"

"Before the war, sir, my father had a company that manufactured safes. Now they make ammunition," Vera said. Brakes raised an eyebrow; it seemed Vera might be more useful than he had anticipated.

"Oh, I see," Brakes said with a stiff nod. "Then get on the phone and get them down here, please."

At his request, Vera frowned. "That would take some time, Inspector," she replied, averting Brakes' gaze. "They live on the Scottish boarder."

Brakes swore under his breath at this new understanding. "Blast it. I'll have to ring the station and ask them to send for someone, then." Scowling, he turned away from the safe and glanced around the office before turning back to Vera with a sigh.

"We'll get someone in," he promised with a nod. "But first, let's search the room."

"Inspector, I'm confused—you tell me to keep my nose out of your investigation. Then, when it suits you, you ask me to help. I need to know where I stand on this?" Vera asked accusingly with her hands perched on her hips.

"Vera, you have proven that you have a keen eye for details; if I choose to exploit that from time to time, then so be it." Brakes replied, gesturing to Vera to start looking around.

Brakes and Vera began combing through the study, searching for anything that might provide a clue. While Brakes inspected the bookshelves for hidden compartments or loose sheets of paper, Vera checked the drawers for anything that might seem out of place.

Suddenly, Vera called out, "Sir, come look at this."

Brakes crossed the room to see what she'd found. Vera held up a crumpled piece of paper from the bottom of one of the desk drawers. It was half torn but legible. Written in a jagged scrawl were the words:

Meet at the old tower. Midnight. No excuses, or it's over.

Brakes' pulse quickened. "The old tower," he whispered. "That could be the abandoned watchtower just outside the city, near the marshlands. It's isolated, perfect for a secret meeting."

Ann, who had been quietly watching the investigation from the doorway, walked over to Brakes and looked at the note. Her face drained of colour.

"I remember now... He left the house that night," Ann murmured, re-reading the note as if searching for her own answers. "Late, after a phone call. He didn't say where he was going, but I heard him leave."

Brakes folded the note carefully, and his thoughts began to race. "Is that where John was murdered?" He asked himself quietly.

Vera's eyes widened. "If we search the tower, we might find more evidence."

"Then we need to move fast," Brakes agreed. "I will ring the station to get someone to open the safe. Once they're finished, I will have them take both Ann and Rosie back to the station."

"Excuse me," Ann cleared her throat and stepped forward. "But why would Rosie need to come to the station?"

Turning, Brakes looked at Ann. "Because I say so, and I also have some questions for her," he said simply, then adds, "You will both stay here and await the officer's arrival and go with them to the station. Vera and I will return once we have searched the site. Understood?"

A mixture of fear, understanding and guilt filled Ann's eyes. Silently, she nodded her agreement.

"Good," Brakes said and, turning to the door, left with Vera hot on his heels. Before leaving the estate, he made sure to use Ann's house phone to call the station with his instructions regarding the safe and informing the officer that they would find Ann and Rosie handcuffed to the staircase.

With the officers on their way to the Marsh estate, Brakes' next destination loomed in the distance as he slid into the passenger seat next to Vera.

He only hoped that the old watchtower would yield yet another puzzle piece in the mystery that was John Marsh's murder.

CHAPTER SIX

It wasn't long before Brakes and Vera arrived at the watchtower. It was still light out, yet the place was empty; it seemed not even the most rambunctious of youths dared come this far outside of the city.

Getting out of the car, Brakes placed a hand atop his hat, just in case the wind picked up.

"Search the grounds," he instructed Vera as she slammed the door shut behind her. "I'll take a look inside. If you hear or find anything, come find me."

Brakes walked towards the watchtower and left Vera to her own devices. Thankfully, she seemed quite eager to have something to do outside of driving, which meant Brakes would find some peace inside while he searched for clues. Once inside, he took his time making sure to inspect every crevice and every splintered piece of wood on the ground.

Strangely, everything inside seemed untouched. There had been no signs of a struggle, no blood splattered on the ground or walls. Even the thick layer of dust within the watchtower had been left undisturbed, the only sign of new life was made by Brakes' footprints.

After a while, he came outside to find Vera still combing the area, her sharp eyes carefully making note of anything and everything she came across. Clearing his throat, Brakes called to her.

"Anything?" He asked. Vera looked up and, almost regretfully, she shook her head.

"Nothing," she called back. At her answer, Brakes sighed almost begrudgingly and gave a solemn nod.

"Let's get back to the station, Vera," he said, striding towards the car. Vera was soon behind him and sliding into the driver's seat, her demeanour slightly deflated compared to before.

As she pulled away from the watchtower, Brakes turned to watch the marshlands pass him by, a frown on his face. The watchtower must have simply been a meeting place and nothing more, he decided. For who—or what—though, Brakes couldn't be sure; all he knew was that it only seemed to be adding to a never-ending list of unanswered questions.

Ann Marsh Second Interview

Brakes made his way back to the interview room where Ann Marsh sat waiting, her face pale and drawn. Brakes took the seat across from her, the weight of the moment settling between them.

The silence was finally broken when Brakes made a clear statement to Ann.

"I'm getting tired of your little truths, Miss Marsh. I know you're misleading me; now, give me the full story." A loud clatter filled the room as Brakes slammed his good hand down on the table in frustration.

Ann took a moment. Her hands trembled in her lap as she began to worry her lip between her teeth while Brakes stayed silent, waiting.

Methodically, he began tapping a finger against the table while he watched Ann, how her eyes seemed to dart between her hands and him, as if she were trying to think of what to say next. Almost as if she were trying to think of a new story to spin.

What Ann did not know, however, was that Brakes knew she was hiding something. It was in how little she spoke, and in all the secrets that lay behind her eyes.

After a short period of silence between them, Brakes re-iterated his question.

"This is your last chance, Ann," he sighed. Ann finally looked up at him, fear clear in her eyes. "Tell me the full story, or you will be charged for the murder of your brother."

Ann's eyes grew even wider. Fidgeting in her chair, she looked down at the table before bringing her hands up to rub her face. Brakes was certain he could hear a shuddering hitch of breath, and watched how her body began to tremble. When she finally removed her hands to look back up at him, Brakes could see the beginning of tears in her eyes.

"Alright. Alright," she whispered, her voice trembling. "I didn't murder my brother, but..."

Brakes leaned across the table. "But...?" He urged her to continue.

Ann chewed on her lip, contemplating her next words. Then, "We did move his body."

Brakes blinked. He had not been expecting Ann to admit such a thing. "*We*?" He asked, knowing well who Ann meant, but he needed her to confirm his suspicions.

"Rosie and I," Ann confirmed. Brakes watched a tear slip down Ann's pale cheek as she recalled the night of her brother's murder. "We were awoken early that morning by a vehicle. There were slamming doors. Loud voices."

Brakes sat a little straighter in his seat, his own eyes growing wide. His suspicions had been correct: Ann had been keeping something from him, and now he had a reason to keep a closer eye on her.

He would not divulge this new plan of action to her, of course. Instead, he pressed for more answers, hoping that this would be the breakthrough he had been looking for.

"Did you recognise anyone?" He asked, leaning across the table. "Get the registration of the vehicle?"

He held his breath as Ann shook her head and lifted a delicate hand to wipe her tears.

"No. It was too dark," she whispered with a sniff. "We watched from my bedroom window. There were three of them. At that point, neither Rosie nor I knew what was going on. All we saw were dark figures, and that they were carrying a body."

Fresh tears spilled down her cheeks as Ann shuddered at the memory. Brakes didn't dare move, waiting with bated breath for Ann to continue. After a moment, Ann tilted her head up to gaze at the ceiling and let out a quivering breath.

"They placed him—the body—over the fountain wall, face down in the water. One of them held his head down while the other two held his arms. They didn't let go until he stopped kicking."

Brakes balled his good hand into a fist and slammed it against the table again. "So, you witnessed the murder of your brother but decided to withhold this information?" He accused, his voice sharp. Ann jumped but, a moment later, her gaze hardened. Standing from her seat, she wiped her eyes with the back of her hand and placed her other hand on her hip as she glared back at Brakes.

"We didn't *know* it was my brother at that point," she insisted, and began pacing the length of the room. "In fact, it wasn't until thirty minutes or so after the men had left that we managed to pluck up the courage to go outside and see who it was."

Flipping open his notebook, Brakes nodded and wrote everything down. The sound of his pencil scratching against the paper and Ann's intermittent sniffling punctuated the air.

"Okay. So, you waited until they left and went outside." Looking up from his notebook, he returned Ann's gaze. "Then what happened?" He asked, tapping his pencil against the paper. Swallowing, Ann continued.

"The body was... it was slumped against the side of the fountain wall when we finally saw him.

We—we pushed him upright. Got a look at his fa…"
Shaken, Ann collapsed back into her seat and clapped
a hand to her mouth, muffling a choked sob. Reaching
into his pocket, Brakes took out a handkerchief and
offered it to the woman. With a small, grateful nod,
Ann took it and began dabbing at her eyes.

"It's alright, Miss Marsh," Brakes mumbled,
before saying something he hardly meant. "Take your
time."

That only seemed to make her sob harder, her
wails bouncing off the walls. Pressing a hand to his
head, Brakes sighed; he dearly wished that she would
stop crying. Of course, he understood that Ann was
reliving a rather terrifying experience, but her
incessant weeping was taking up time that could be
spent out on the field. Still, he kept a level-head; if he
rushed the poor woman, then Brakes might miss
pertinent information.

Finally, after what might have been longer than
necessary, Ann's sobs quietened.

"There was blood. Bruises. It was horrible," she
whispered, her face even paler than Brakes had
thought possible. "I barely recognised him. But it was
John. My brother. My brother was dead, in our
fountain."

Ann's eyes, bluer than Brakes had ever seen
them, welled with fresh tears. Her lips formed in a
small 'o', but no words came out while she looked off
into the distance. She sat there, completely silent

while Brakes nodded, continuing to jot down everything Ann had revealed.

"So, you have just discovered your brother's body," Brakes reiterated, going over his notes. "Why didn't you call the police?" He looked back up at Ann. Immediately, a flash of anger crossed her features.

"We were in shock," she snapped furiously. "We weren't *thinking* straight. My brother had just been killed in front of us. I..." Ann stopped and once again, her eyes filled with horror.

"What?" Brakes asked, nearly jumping from his seat. "What have you remembered, Miss Marsh?"

"I—I saw it," she whispered, eyes falling to the table as she slumped back in her seat. "I saw it. Then I removed it. I couldn't let anyone see..."

"Saw what? What did you see, Miss Marsh?" Brakes leaned in further. Before long, he would practically be lying on the table.

Blinking, it was as if Ann had seen a ghost when she finally said, "The piece of paper they nailed to his chest."

It was Brakes' turn to fall silent, understanding settling upon him. So, that was why there had been holes in John Marsh's chest. The murderers must have used the rusty nails after they had killed him. Or, worse—they had done it moments before Marsh had been killed, as a means of torture, perhaps?

"What was written on it?" Brakes asked, eager to know more. "And why did you remove the evidence, Miss Marsh?"

"They had written one word in large, red letters. Just one," she explained, her voice seeming even more frail. "I had to remove it. My family couldn't have another scandal, you see."

Ann shook her head again and squeezed her eyes shut, as if banishing the memory of her brother's body from her mind. Brakes, however, had no time for Ann's dramatics.

"You still haven't told me what was written on it," Brakes growled, aware that he was pressing Ann for answers she was unwilling to give. She glared at him, her lips pressing into a thin line as she balled the handkerchief in her fist.

"It was just that one, horrible word, pinned to his chest with nails," she hissed, bringing a hand to her mouth. "Sorry, I—I can't bring myself to say it."

Brakes let out an intelligible sound of annoyance. "Well, if you can't say it, can you at least write it down, woman?" He barked. Thankfully, Ann nodded.

"I can do that," she whispered, chewing on the edge of her thumbnail. Quickly, Brakes tore off a blank slip of paper from his notebook and slid it across the table to Ann and threw a pencil in her direction.

Leaning down, Ann hastily scribbled the word before sliding the note paper and pencil towards a waiting Brakes. He pounced, fresh understanding barely in his grasp as he took the paper and stared at the very word that seemed to horrify Ann so. And there, written in a shaken script, was the word:

PUFFTER

Brakes looked up at Ann, her gaze once again on the table. Folding the piece of paper, he slipped it into his pocket and stood from his chair.

"Thank you, Miss Marsh," he said, and cleared his throat to excuse himself from the room. Promptly, he went to find a pair of uniformed officers.

"Go and find Miss Marsh's maid, Rosie, and bring her to the station," he instructed the officers. "I want you to keep a close guard over her."

Brakes made his way to the break room and made a couple cups of tea before returning to the interview room. Passing Ann a cup, he watched as she wrapped her trembling hands around it and took in its warmth. Sitting back down, Brakes did a short overview of what Ann had told him thus far before asking her to continue.

"Well, you see, I couldn't allow his body to be found. Not with that... *word* on his chest," she replied bitterly. Nursing the cup between her hands, Ann continued. "Our family has already had one scandal regarding *that* matter, back in our school days. No.

So, Rosie and I removed it. The nails, too. I threw them in the fire, in the parlour."

Brakes made a few more notes on his sheets. Taking a short moment to gather his thoughts, he then asked Ann,

"At that point, did he still have his false leg?"

"Well, it wasn't until I decided that we should move the body off the estate, that I realised his leg was missing," Ann explained with a shake of her head. "Rosie and I tried to pick him up, but she—she screamed. Said that his leg was missing."

Ann fell quiet again while Brakes continued writing down his notes. Looking up, he raised a brow, waiting for her to continue. She didn't.

"Okay, so his leg was missing," he said slowly, making sure Ann knew he had been listening. "What did you do next?"

"I asked Rosie to go and get the truck from the back of the house," she explained, her voice growing smaller and smaller. "Whilst she was gone, I—I held John and apologised to him for what we were about to do."

Brakes paused, taking everything in before concluding what had transpired next.

"Right. So, Rosie arrived with the truck, you both loaded his body and drove to the vicarage, then dumped his body," Brakes stated, earning him a nod from Ann. "Yet that does not explain how you two girls, small in frame, lifted your brother's body onto the truck before dumping it, Miss Marsh. Not to mention, you did not leave any tyre tracks."

"Well, we didn't actually do that part," Ann admitted, and she had the decency to look ashamed. "I paid a couple of estate men to undergo *that* particular task. He was far too heavy for us to pick up, you see."

Brakes sighed. Taking off his hat, he rubbed his temples; at least he was getting somewhere, he told himself. Still, it seemed as if Ann was determined to complicate matters further, though deep down, it made sense that she could not have disposed of her own brother's body without the aid of a man or two.

"Wasn't it enough for both you and Rosie to tamper with the crime scene?" He groaned with a shake of his head. "And now you tell me that you have involved two other people? I will require their names, Miss Marsh."

Ann provided the two men's names and Brakes made a note of them. Looking over his papers, Brakes could see the beginnings of a partial crime scene were beginning to form—the fountain on the estate where John was killed, and the missing paper that had been nailed to his chest, either before or after he had been drowned. Three men, still unknown, holding him down.

Yet there were still questions left unanswered.

Where did this all start? *Why* did it start, and who were those three men? Where was John's false leg, and why did he have two pieces of envelope in his sock?

"You will remain at the station until further notice," Brakes informed Ann as he pushed his chair back to stand. "And Miss Marsh? Know that you may well be charged for tampering with a crime scene. Good day."

Tipping his hat, Brakes turned his back on Ann just as the beginnings of fresh tears filled her eyes. Soft hiccups and sobs began to fill the room again as Brakes left, making sure to instruct one of the nearby uniformed officers to take her back to a cell and stand guard over her.

Turning a corner, Brakes entered the room where the maid, Rosie, was being held. It looked like she had been crying, too, but that did little to waver his resolve.

"Right, Rosie—as you are aware, we have Ann here also. I have just finished her second interview, and she has now given me the full story regarding what you both did with John's body." Brakes pulled out a chair and sat down. "Now, you have a choice; make it easy on yourself and give me your full story or try lying to me."

Rosie instantly burst into tears, her small body beginning to shake uncontrollably.

"What is going to happen to me?" She asked, her voice rising with each word. Brakes simply shrugged.

"That all depends on your candour right here, right now."

Taking out her handkerchief, Rosie wiped her eyes and then her nose, before calming herself down enough to confirm Ann's account of that terrible night.

"You will be held in custody for your part in helping Miss Marsh," he explained plainly. And with that, Brakes exited the room and made his way through the station, ignoring Rosie's rising sobs.

Once he found Vera, he instructed her to bring the car round before heading towards the Chief's office. Once he had given the Chief a debrief of the investigation as requested, Brakes made his way out of the station to a waiting Vera.

Vera drove Brakes back to the Marsh estate, the early morning mist still lingering over the countryside like a veil of secrets. She stopped just short of the fountain, careful not to disturb the scene.

The fountain stood like a silent sentinel in the centre of the estate's grounds, its water trickling gently as if mocking the violence that had occurred there not long ago.

Brakes stepped out of the car, his face set in a look of grim determination. The events from the previous day had shaken him, but there was no room for doubt now. He motioned for Vera to join him, and she jumped out, closing the door softly behind her.

"Come over here, Vera," he instructed, opening the boot of the car. He retrieved two pairs of rubber gloves, his trusty magnifying glass, and a few glass tubes. He smiled faintly as he handed one pair of gloves to her.

"Sir, yes sir!" She replied enthusiastically, though her voice carried a mix of nerves and excitement.

"I know you're not trained for this," Brakes began, giving her a glance, "but two sets of eyes are better than one. Stay behind me and be careful where you step, and don't touch anything without your gloves on."

Vera nodded, slipping the gloves on as they approached the fountain. Brakes crouched by the edge of the fountain, meticulously collecting a water sample in one of the glass tubes. He made a quick note in his small notebook before handing the sample to Vera.

Just then, Brakes was interrupted by a man coming out of the house—it was the safe cracker, carrying a bunch of papers in his hands.

"It took a while to open, but I got there in the end, Inspector," the man said, his voice low. "Here are the contents; just family papers, and not much else." Handing them over to Brakes, the safe cracker threw his bag over his shoulder, jumped on his push-bike and left.

Brakes, though disappointed, gave the papers a quick scan. The safe cracker was right; nothing at all of interest in them. Handing them over to Vera, Brakes asked her to bag them up with the other evidence they had accrued so far.

Brakes' keen eyes scanned the area between the fountain and the house, inspecting the gravel with his magnifying glass. Sure enough, as Ann had described, there were traces of blood, soaked into the gravel like a sinister imprint of what had transpired. He collected a small sample, carefully sealing it in another glass tube before passing it to Vera.

"No signs of a struggle on the fountain itself, though," Brakes muttered, inspecting the smooth stone. "But that's not surprising if the people involved were dressed in soft clothing."

He straightened up, gazing thoughtfully at the ground. "If you were being drowned here, you'd struggle, wouldn't you?"

"I believe so, sir. Yes," Vera replied, watching his every move.

"Right," Brakes said, looking down at the gravel. "Let's see if we can find any signs beneath the surface. Start pulling back the gravel—carefully."

They worked in silence, the only sound in the air being the soft scrape of gravel being moved. After a few painstaking minutes, they uncovered several deep foot impressions, right at the base of the fountain. Brakes knelt down, examining the impressions closely. They weren't typical footprints—more like heavy indentations where feet had been forced into the ground, resisting something. It seemed likely that they were made through the violent act of being held under water.

"There," Brakes said, pointing. "Two distinct marks. Boots or shoes, about three feet apart. Whoever it was put up a fight, no doubt."

He traced a line in the gravel with his finger, a long drag mark leading away from the fountain. "Likely from John's missing prosthetic."

Vera's eyes widened as she glanced over at Brakes. Nodding, he stood up and brushed off his trousers.

"It matches Ann's description and what we've found. There was someone powerful enough to drown him, but John fought back, even with one leg."

They worked in sync after that, photographing the scene and collecting the final pieces of evidence. Once everything was loaded into the car, they headed back to the station. Vera was still buzzing with questions, her excitement palpable, but Brakes could feel the weight of the case pressing down on him.

The drive back was tense, but Vera couldn't help herself any longer. "Sir, that kit you've got in the boot—is that something you put together?"

Brakes gave a small smile, his eyes fixed on the road. "No, Vera. It's standard issue. Back in the late 1920s, Scotland Yard and Sir Bernard Spilsbury developed it. Every detective carries one now."

Silence followed, but only for a moment.

"Do you think Ann killed her own brother?" Vera blurted out, her question a mixture of curiosity and disbelief.

Brakes' jaw tightened. He'd warned her before about asking too many questions, but he understood her need to make sense of things.

"I've asked you not to speculate, Vera," he growled, fixing her with a stern look. "I have let you help with the mundane parts of the investigation, but you need to know when to hold your tongue."

Vera's face fell, but Brakes could tell by her raised eyebrow that she would certainly keep on speculating. He sighed, deciding to let it go; there were bigger things to focus on, after all, such as the next round of interviews and the mounting evidence that seemed to lead him in circles.

Back at the station, Brakes retrieved the samples and camera from the boot of the car and handed them to Vera. "Take these down to the lads in the basement. Make sure the blood sample is processed first and have them develop the photos."

While Vera rushed off, Brakes poured himself a cup of tea, savouring the brief moment of quiet. A few minutes later, out of the corner of his eye, he spotted Vera returning to the room where she immediately started talking to the WAPC making a cup of tea. His temper flared.

"VERA!" He bellowed, causing the squad room to fall into a deafening silence at his resounding cry. "Leave that WAPC alone!"

Vera jumped, startled, and turned toward him with a look of wide-eyed confusion. Brakes motioned for her to follow him into a side room. Once inside, he slammed the door behind them, his frustration boiling over.

"I'm getting sick of your meddling, Vera," Brakes snapped, spittle beginning to fly with each word. "I don't mind you helping with some aspects of the case, but you simply cannot go on asking questions or talking to others regarding this case! I'll be asking for a new driver first thing tomorrow."

"Sir!" Vera protested urgently. "I wasn't asking about the case! We were just talking about the differences between the WAPC and the ATS."

Brakes blinked, his anger cooling as realisation dawned on him. He had wrongly accused her. She hadn't been overstepping, and now he felt foolish. He took a deep breath, rubbing his temples.

"Apologies, Vera," he murmured regretfully. "This case... it's getting to me. I'm not usually like this."

Thankfully, Vera accepted his apology without hesitation. The sting of his words still lingered, though, that much was obvious. Brakes, in an attempt to smooth things over further, gave her a task.

"I need you to go to the *Norwich Post*," he instructed. "Find out everything you can about any Marsh family scandal from a few years back. There's something we're missing."

At this, Vera perked up. "Yes, sir," she replied, her eyes bright with renewed purpose.

As she left, Brakes collected his thoughts. He needed to talk to Ann again. But first, he had to bring the Chief up to speed on what they had uncovered.

CHAPTER SEVEN

Arriving at the cottages where the Marsh estate workers lived, DI Brakes approached the scene with a calculated calm. He wasn't expecting much cooperation—in his experience, workers like these were often loyal to their employers, or simply didn't want to get involved in a police investigation. This particular case felt no different.

Interviewing the two men separately yielded little—both denied any involvement in the removal of John Marsh's body, and neither provided information about the gruesome discovery of the missing leg.

Brakes knew they were lying. The subtle avoidance of eye contact, the rigid posture—these men had something to hide.

"You leave me no choice but to arrest you both for tampering with a crime scene," he said, taking out two pairs of cuffs and cuffing the men. Thankfully, they both complied without issue.

Vera arrived with the car just as Brakes had finished jotting down some notes and put the two men into the back of the vehicle. As he closed the door behind them, Vera stepped out of the car and handed Brakes a copy of an old newspaper. She pointed to an article she had found in the *Norwich Post* archives.

"I think you will find this interesting," she said simply. Brakes looked it over and with an agreeing nod opened the passenger seat door.

"Right, let's get these two to the station and booked in. Then we will deal with this," Brakes said, and Vera jumped back into to the car.

Once they had deposited the two men at the station, Brakes returned to the car, which was still running.

"Main house then, sir, is it?" Vera asked, though it was clear she already knew the answer.

"Yes, let's go—I want to take another look around that place."

The sprawling estate loomed large. Its grand architecture juxtaposed against the unease Brakes felt about what waited inside. As they neared the entrance, the front door stood ajar. Faint voices— raised and distinctly female—floated toward them.

Brakes motioned for Vera to follow him. They walked into the sunroom where the source of the argument was immediately clear: Ann Marsh and Rosie were locked in a heated dispute. Ann's face was flushed with anger, and her hands gestured wildly as she argued with her companion.

Though surprised to see Ann and Rosie there, Brakes gathered himself and cleared his throat. He was, of course, ignored. So, with a booming, authoritative bellow, Brakes yelled,

"*Ladies!*" Immediately, he captured their attention, their argument cut short.

Both women turned sharply toward him, startled by his sudden presence. With Vera hovering behind him like a protective shadow, they must have appeared to the women like a two-headed beast.

"Sit down," Brakes instructed, waving them toward the chairs. His tone brooked no argument, and the women, still bristling with tension, complied.

"Firstly, Ann—what are you doing home?" Brakes asked, still confused by her presence. "Who released you?"

"Your Chief. He apparently needed the cells," Ann explained begrudgingly. "One of your officers is around here somewhere, as Rosie and I are under house arrest, now."

As Ann settled into her chair, Brakes pulled the folded newspaper from his pocket. It had taken Vera hours of digging through archives to find the article, but now he was holding a vital piece to unravelling the mystery behind John Marsh's murder. He handed the paper to Ann, tapping it once for emphasis.

"Explain this, Miss Marsh."

The headline was as damning as it was old, and Ann's eyes darkened the moment she saw it. Without reading further, she slammed the paper on the table. "That was a long time ago," she snapped. "Teenagers do foolish things, Inspector. It's hardly relevant to my brother's murder."

Brakes leaned in, his gaze steady. "Relevant enough, I'd say. We all go through phases, Miss Marsh, but this particular 'phase' paints an interesting picture. It seems your brother's sexual identity wasn't so secret after all. What if someone in this community took exception to it?"

Ann remained silent, but her jaw clenched—a sign Brakes took as confirmation that they were closer to the truth than she'd like to admit.

"Your brother was gay," Brakes continued, "and it seems someone wanted to send a message. His death wasn't random—it was calculated, personal."

"But why now?" Ann shot back, her voice wavering. "After all these years, why would someone decide to kill John over this?"

Brakes' eyes flicked toward the window, lost in thought. The question lingered, as did the unsettling notion that John's death was just the surface of a deeper, more intricate plot.

Before he could respond, the family lawyer arrived, visibly tense. "Inspector. I need to speak with my client regarding John Marsh's death," the lawyer insisted, his tone final. Brakes stood up, fixing Ann with a final, hard look.

"I'll be back, Miss Marsh. There are still many questions you need to answer," he said before taking his leave.

The Chase

The ride back to the station was quiet at first, but Vera's mounting frustration was palpable. She fidgeted with the steering wheel, muttering under her breath.

"Alright, Vera," Brakes exhaled, unable to take the silence any longer. "Spit it out."

Vera shot him a glance, then finally voiced what had been troubling her. "Do you really think John was killed because of... you know, his sexual activities?"

"It's possible," Brakes replied, though the uncertainty in his tone hinted at his own doubts. "People have been killed for less, especially in places like this, where prejudices run deep."

Vera sighed, shaking her head. "It doesn't sit right with me, sir. There has to be more to it."

Brakes didn't disagree. The case gnawed at him, especially the missing leg. Something about it didn't fit neatly into a simple hate crime narrative. Why take the leg? What did it symbolise—or worse, what was it hiding?

Suddenly, Vera jerked the car to the left, narrowly avoiding a motorcycle that had sped out of an alleyway. Immediately, Brakes recognised the riders as the same young thieves who had been causing trouble all over town.

"Follow them!" Brakes yelled. Vera didn't hesitate; dropping the car into a lower gear, she accelerated with a precision that left Brakes gripping his seat. The motorcycle zigzagged through the narrow streets, the riders desperate to escape, but Vera was relentless. A police car roared down cobblestone roads, its bell wailing as pedestrians scrambled out of the way.

The chase intensified as the motorcycle veered sharply into a narrow alleyway, one too tight for Vera's vehicle. Screeching to a halt, she slammed the steering wheel in frustration as the motorcycle disappeared from view.

"Damn it!" Brakes cursed, pounding the dashboard with his good hand.

Two uniformed officers who had witnessed the chase approached the car moments later. "Close one, inspector," one of them said with a shake of his head.

Brakes' jaw clenched, his body stiffening in frustration. "I'll get those little bastards. They're not slipping through my fingers again," Brakes growled.

The two officers started to move away from the car again. Just as Brakes leaned back to collect himself, the air filled with the sharp sound of police whistles.

"Could be them," Vera murmured, her eyes growing wide with anticipation. Without another word, Vera threw the car into reverse and sped toward the commotion. It was clear that she had a talent for driving—something Brakes seldom acknowledged, given Vera's penchant for accidents—however, in a moment such as this, it was impossible to ignore.

They navigated the twisting streets with ease, arriving just in time to see a young girl being held by an officer. The second Vera pulled up, Brakes jumped out of the car.

"What've you got?" He asked, eyeing the girl.

"Just a petty thief, sir. Stole some apples from the market," the officer explained.

Brakes glanced at the girl's small, dirty hands clutching the apples. She couldn't have been more than eleven, her face streaked with grime and cheeks hollow from hunger.

He sighed, nodding to Vera. "Let her go. Pay the stall owner for the apples and send her on her way."

The officer, though reluctant, released the girl. Brakes knelt on one knee in front of the girl and asked,

"Have you seen anything unusual on the streets recently? A fight involving several men, maybe?"

"I saw a man. He had a bad leg… he was limping," she replied in a quivering voice.

"And?" Brakes asked, encouraging the girl to continue.

"Two men grabbed him and took him up an alley."

Brakes leaned closer. "Show me."

The girl led them to a narrow alley where she claimed the attack had occurred. Brakes scanned the area with laser focus, his eyes sweeping over every detail. Halfway down, he found something—a single button, torn from a jacket.

It wasn't much, but it was more than he'd had before, and now he had yet another crime scene involving the Marsh murder to consider. Two scenes showing signs of a struggle, and one that was the murder scene. What the hell was going on?

Returning to the car, Brakes instructed Vera to drive him down to Peterborough. Maybe Miss Marsden could shed more light on the situation.

Peterborough

Later that evening, they drove to Peterborough to interview Jenny Marsden, the only person left on Brakes' list. Brakes couldn't shake the feeling that the case was starting to get more blurred by the moment.

Vera pulled down a narrow street, carefully navigating down the road whilst Brakes looked for the right house number. It was mid-afternoon, and the street was full of kids. Boys playing football, girls skipping with a rope, kids playing chase—Vera had to keep a sharp eye on them, especially when they were playing on the road.

Two thirds of the way down, Brakes asked her to pull over. "You wait here, Vera."

Brakes made his way toward the house. Knocking on the door, he was met by an old man wearing a white t-shirt. It looked like it had the whole of last weeks' dinner stains dotted down the front, and one of the straps from his braces hung loosely off his left shoulder.

"Can I help you?" The man asked.

Brakes introduced himself and showed his identification before asking, "Does Miss Jenny Marsden Live here, and if so, could I have a word with her, please?"

With a grunt, the man swung the door open wider and gestured Brakes toward the back of the house.

Brakes found himself in the kitchen where a young lady stood at the sink, washing vegetables. She looked up the moment he entered, and Brakes introduced himself again.

"Are you Miss Jenny Marsden?" He asked, his voice authoritative.

"Yes," she replied, wiping her hands on her pinny.

"Good. I need to talk to you about John Marsh," Brakes began. He didn't wait for her reaction and went straight to the point. "I am sorry, but I have to inform you that he is dead." At this news, Jenny seemed to stumble, and her face turned pale.

She was silent for a moment, processing the words. Finally, she managed to form the question that was on her mind.

"Alcohol poisoning, was it?" She asked. Brakes shook his head.

"No, he was murdered." Brakes frowned and his tone turned grim. "I understand you were in a relationship with him for some time. What can you tell me about him?"

Jenny's eyes widened as she pondered over Brakes' words, and she grew silent. It did not take long for her to offer him an answer, though.

"Not a lot, really. Our relationship lasted one week—he was a very troubled man, you see," Jenny explained with a sigh. "Haunted not just by his accident and the loss of his parents, but also his twin brother, who died in the accident, too. I guess that's why he drank so much." She paused, as if trying to find more to say. Finally, she shook her head. "That's all I can tell you really, Inspector."

Brakes nodded and jotted down some notes in his pad. He closed it and slipped it back into his jacket pocket.

"Thank you. It seems you learned quite a bit about him in such a short time," Brakes remarked. Jenny simply shrugged.

"He drank a lot. He would get emotional and say things, over and over. And that false leg wasn't just for keeping him upright," she said, wringing her hands together. At this, Brakes visibly perked up. Was this another piece to an ever-growing puzzle?

"What do you mean?" He asked, urging Jenny to keep talking. "About his leg, that is."

"It was hollow, a great place to hide things. Often acted like a courier for anyone willing to pay," she offered, her voice low. "You might want to look closer at his so-called friends, too—not very nice people at all." Jenny paused again, but it seemed she had now expelled all her knowledge on John Marsh. "Now, if that's all, I am sorry, but I really have to go to work. You can find your own way out."

Jenny quickly pushed past Brakes and headed upstairs, while he headed straight for the door, his mind beginning to race.

As it turned out, John seemed to have connections to a variety of unsavoury characters, according to Jenny Marsden. From what he had gleaned from Jenny's account, John Marsh had also been involved in smuggling and had used his prosthetic leg to transport illegal goods.

As Brakes walked back to the car, he felt the weight of the case pressing down on him. John Marsh's death wasn't just a hate crime; it was now something far more dangerous.

"Right, Vera," Brakes said once he returned to the car. "Let's find a pub."

It didn't take long to find one. Taking a deep breath, Brakes allowed the warm pub atmosphere to settle over him. The hum of quiet conversation from the other patrons seemed miles away, lost under the weight of the revelations Jenny had shared.

Vera went to fetch them both a drink while Brakes sat down, replaying the details of his conversation with Jenny in his head.

Minutes later, his untouched pint sat in front of him, the condensation from the glass pooling on the table. Vera sipped her own drink, waiting patiently for him to speak, though the silence between them was almost tangible.

Finally, Brakes broke the quiet. "A twin brother, Vera. Can you believe that? John Marsh had a twin, and nobody saw fit to mention it."

Vera's brow furrowed. "That's strange, sir. I mean, why would his sister leave out such an important detail? Could it have something to do with his murder?"

Brakes sighed, running a hand through his hair. "That's what I'm trying to figure out. Jenny said that John only talked about his brother when he was drunk." He paused, sitting with his thoughts for a moment before continuing. "But people thought he was making it up."

"And you think this might have something to do with his smuggling?" Vera asked.

Brakes leaned back in his chair, his eyes narrowing in thought. "Possibly. It sounds like John's been running with a bad crowd for a while. Using his hollow leg to transport contraband—that's clever, I'll give him that. But cleverness doesn't keep you safe when you're dealing with dangerous people."

Vera leaned in, her voice lowering as if she were afraid someone might overhear. "But sir, what if his leg wasn't just used for smuggling? What if whoever killed him was after something specific? Something hidden inside the leg?"

Brakes tapped the table with his finger, considering her words. It was a theory, and a good one at that. If John Marsh's false leg had been more than just a prosthetic—if it *had* carried something valuable enough to kill for—then it might explain why his leg had been taken after his murder. But what could that be?

"We need to find out more about this smuggling ring," he said, glancing at Vera. "Jenny said John worked as a courier for anyone willing to pay. That means he was a middleman, not the one calling the shots. Whoever he worked for—whoever wanted that leg—they're still out there. And I doubt they're finished."

Vera straightened up, her expression serious. "What's our next move, sir?"

Brakes glanced at the clock behind the bar. "Tomorrow, we'll head back to Norwich. Something doesn't sit right with me. Jenny Marsden seemed genuinely shaken by the news of John's death, but there's more she's not telling me. And I don't trust coincidences. I saw her leave the house in a hurry after I did."

"You think she's hiding something?" Vera asked, raising an eyebrow.

Brakes drained his pint, the tepid liquid finally breaking through the tension in his chest. "Maybe. Or maybe she's just scared."

Later that night, after securing lodgings at a nearby inn, Brakes lay on the stiff mattress, his mind whirling. The details of the case tumbled around in his thoughts like broken shards of glass, none of them quite fitting together. He stared at the cracked ceiling.

John Marsh's murder was brutal, personal. The missing leg, the taunts and fights he endured because of it... there was a message behind this killing, something beyond mere prejudice or hate. Only Brakes wasn't sure yet what that message was, yet.

And now, with the revelation of a twin brother—a brother who had died in the same accident that took their parents—Brakes wondered if that part of John's past held a deeper significance. Could there be a connection between his brother's death and the life John had led? The loss of his family seemed to haunt him, driving him into the underworld, but was there more to it than just grief?

Brakes sighed, rolled his eyes, and turned to stare at the small desk by the window. Tomorrow would bring new challenges. There were still questions he needed to ask Ann and Rosie, and more leads to follow up on. But for now, he needed rest. His body ached from the long day, and the adrenaline that had fuelled him through the chase earlier was finally wearing off.

The next morning, Vera drove Brakes back to Norwich. When they reached the station, he didn't even get a chance to take his coat off before the sergeant stopped him.

"Inspector, there is an urgent message for you," he said stiffly, passing Brakes a piece of paper.

"A witness came forward last night, someone who claims they saw three men, one of them carrying a large object out of an alley near the pub on the night of John's murder."

Brakes felt a jolt of energy shoot through him. "A witness. Three men? And what is this object? John's missing leg, maybe?" He murmured to himself, reading over the note again and again, in case he had missed something.

A smile broke out onto Brakes' face. At last, and about time, something tangible had fallen into his hands.

CHAPTER EIGHT

Vera had just entered the station, ready to take off her driving gloves when Brakes stopped her in her tracks.

"Right, Vera, get the car; I need to go and speak to this witness," he said excitedly. Vera raised an eyebrow.

"Right away, sir," she replied, and went back through the swinging doors.

The streets were busy as they made their way to the address on the statement. People moved about, going through their daily routines. Yet even with the buzz of activity around them, the atmosphere felt strangely subdued. Food rationing and fuel shortages meant that most of the traffic consisted of military vehicles. Private cars were a rarity, with petrol too precious a commodity.

Brakes' gaze wandered as he stared out of the car window, and he couldn't help but notice the contrast between the British and American vehicles that now crowded Norwich. The U.S. trucks and jeeps looked bulkier, more rugged, compared to their British counterparts. But what caught his eye wasn't just the size difference—it was a young man riding a motorcycle, of a similar age to those bag snatchers hitting the city. The motorcycle he was riding was also American. Could he be part of the same gang, Brakes wondered.

"Hold on a minute," Brakes muttered, leaning forward in his seat.

Vera glanced at him curiously. "What is it, sir?"

"That man on the motorcycle," Brakes said, narrowing his eyes. "He's wearing a British uniform, but he's riding an American motorcycle. And his uniform's too big for him. Doesn't add up."

Vera quickly spotted the man he was talking about, and thankfully did not need him to elaborate further. Though she didn't say a word, Brakes could see excitement flicker across her face, her own gaze becoming determined.

"Turn around. Follow him," Brakes instructed, keeping calm.

Without hesitation, Vera performed a quick U-turn and dropped down a couple of gears to catch up to the motorcyclist.

"Who are we after, Inspector?" She asked excitedly, despite already knowing that Brakes didn't have the full answer yet.

"I don't know yet," Brakes replied, fixated on the man ahead. "Just keep your distance. We don't want to spook him."

For the next couple of hours, they followed the young man. Brakes watched carefully as the motorcyclist made stops at various shops and houses around town. Each time, he would get off the bike, his too-large uniform flapping around him, but he never seemed to carry anything with him—no packages, no deliveries, nothing. The whole thing felt strange. Suspicious, even. Brakes jotted down the addresses of each location for later investigation.

Vera glanced over at him as they trailed behind at a safe distance. "Do you think he's part of the gang stealing bags around town, sir?" She asked.

Brakes considered it. The motorcycle matched the description they had received about the bag-snatching incidents, as well as Brakes' own memory from his two run-ins with them.

"It's possible," he replied slowly. "The bike's the same, and he's certainly trying to go unnoticed. Let's just see where he leads us."

They continued to follow him throughout the afternoon. But as the hours dragged on, Brakes couldn't shake the feeling that they were being toyed with. Either the young man had spotted them at some point, or he knew the city streets too well, because he began to weave in and out of alleyways, using the narrower side streets to lose them. By the time they realized what had happened, he was gone.

"Damn it," Brakes muttered, frustrated. "We lost him."

Vera shot him a sympathetic look. "It's getting late. Should I take you home, sir?"

Brakes sighed, leaning back in his seat. "Yeah. We've wasted enough time today."

Back at home, not even a minute had passed by when there was a knock at the door. Upon opening it, Brakes came face to face with a steaming cooking pot.

"I hope you're hungry, Inspector," said a familiar voice from behind the pot. "I have made you a rabbit stew." A friendly smile appeared a moment later, and Brakes was met with his elderly female neighbour.

Brakes took the pot from her hands and thanked her for her kindness. His neighbour would often cook for him and had even washed his clothes several times. It was like having his own mother living next door. But in reality, it was just how the war had made some people; always looking out for their neighbour's, caring and sharing.

Taking the pot over to the stove to warm it, Brakes returned to his thoughts on the day's failings. The missed opportunity with the bag snatching gang gnawed at him, and he could not help but think that it had been a long, fruitless day.

After the stew had warmed on the stove, Brakes ate quickly before changing into his garage clothes and heading out to the garage again. He needed to clear his head, and there was nothing better for that than working on his motorbike.

As he fumbled with the engine parts, his thoughts drifted back to Ann and Rosie. Everything kept leading back to them. He wasn't sure if they were involved in the smuggling operation, but something about them didn't sit right. Tomorrow, he would need to confront them again, dig deeper into their secrets.

The next morning, Brakes was up early. He sipped a strong cup of tea, the early light streaming through the window. His mind felt clearer, the fog of the previous day's frustrations beginning to lift. He was convinced that Ann and Rosie knew more than they were letting on; there was something about the Marsh family, something hidden beneath the surface.

When Vera arrived to pick him up, Brakes instructed her to take him to the witness's house from the other night, then on to the Marsh residence. The drive through town was slow, the streets bustling with market traders and townsfolk going about their day.

As they passed by the market, Brakes found his mind wandering for a moment, watching the routine of the traders as they hawked their goods. The calls of "Potatoes, threepence a pound!" and "Rabbit, sixpence a pound!" filled the air. He smiled briefly. The sounds of the market were familiar, comforting, a reminder that life carried on. The British stiff upper lip would always prevail.

But his reverie was shattered when, at a junction, the back door of the car suddenly flew open. A man jumped into the seat behind them, slamming the door shut.

"What the hell—!" Brakes spun around in his seat, his heart racing.

"Who are you?" Vera gasped, clutching the steering wheel.

"Pull over!" Brakes barked.

Vera swerved to the side of the road, her hands shaking as she brought the car to a halt. Brakes threw open his door, jumped out and proceeded to yank open the rear door to confront the intruder.

"Out!" he growled, grabbing the man by the jacket and throwing him out onto the pavement. His fury rose when the man knocked his hat from his head, flattening Brakes' beloved fedora in the process.

"Stay there!" he snapped at the man as Brakes snatched up his hat, his hands trembling while he reshaped it with care. Muttering under his breath, Brakes inhaled deeply, calming himself. Vera watched from the car and shook her head.

Brakes turned back to the man sprawled on the pavement. "Now, explain yourself."

He proceeded to glare down at the man, who was now trying to prop himself up and brush dust from his rumpled jacket. The stranger, though not particularly large, had a wiry build, and his clothes hung loosely off him as if he had recently lost weight. His face was pale, and sweat had started to bead on his forehead despite the cool morning air.

"Well?" Brakes barked. "I don't have all day. Who the hell are you, and what do you think you're doing, jumping into my car like that?"

The man's eyes darted around nervously. The man, now up on one knee, looked like he was about to bolt, as if he was just waiting for the starting pistol. But the sight of Brakes' sharp gaze and the sturdy figure of Vera at the wheel seemed to pin the man in place.

"Please," the man stammered, holding up his hands in a gesture of surrender. "I didn't mean to startle you. I—I had no choice."

"No choice?" Brakes repeated, his tone incredulous. "You had no choice but to throw yourself into my car and nearly give my driver a heart attack?"

Vera, still gripping the wheel but now more composed, let out a sharp breath. "It was quite the surprise, I'll say that much."

Brakes advanced a step, looming over the man. "Start talking. Who are you, and why did you think it was a good idea to jump into a police inspector's car?"

The man swallowed hard, his Adam's apple bobbing in his throat. "Name's Peter. Peter Oakes," he said quickly. "I knew it was your car, Inspector. I just—I thought you could help me. I'm in trouble. Big trouble. Have you read my statement I left at the station the other night?" he asked desperately.

Brakes paused and looked over to Vera. It seemed his witness had fallen right into his lap. Turning back to the man in question, Brakes offered him a stiff nod.

"Yes, I have read it. We were just on our way to see you." Brakes raised an eyebrow, feeling sceptical. "Trouble, eh? You don't say."

Peter looked nervous, his eyes wide and fearful. With quivering hands, he reached for Brakes and, with a trembling voice, whispered,

"Please, Inspector. I've been followed for days now. They're watching me. I've got nowhere else to go."

Brakes leaned back, crossing his arms while he studied Peter Oakes. The man's desperation was deep, but Brakes had seen enough liars and crooks in his time to know that desperation didn't always mean innocence.

"Who's watching you?" Brakes asked, his voice cold but probing. "And why?"

Peter licked his lips nervously, his eyes darting down the street as if expecting someone to leap out at any moment. "I—I don't know who they are, but I know they've got something to do with the Marsh family. That's why I came to you. You're investigating them, aren't you? I've seen you at the Marsh estate."

Brakes stiffened at the mention of the Marsh family. So, this wasn't a random encounter after all. He exchanged a quick glance with Vera, who frowned but kept her thoughts to herself.

"You saw me at the Marsh estate?" Brakes asked, his tone turning more cautious. "How exactly would you know that I was there?"

Peter hesitated, then shifted uncomfortably. "I've been watching the Marshes for weeks now. I'm not the only one being followed, Inspector. There's something going on—something big." Peter fell quiet for a moment, his gaze shifting once again, before continuing. "I can't get involved, but I need your protection. I swear, I can tell you things... things you don't know about John Marsh's death."

Brakes' head snapped back with surprise at the mention of John Marsh. He wasn't sure if Peter Oakes was being honest, but any lead was better than none at this point.

"Get in the car," Brakes said abruptly, jerking his head toward the backseat. "We'll talk. But if you try anything, anything at all, you'll regret it."

Peter didn't need to be told twice. He hurried back into the car, sliding into the seat he had been ejected from moments earlier. Brakes rounded the car and got in beside Vera, who was still eyeing their new passenger suspiciously.

"Take us somewhere quiet, Vera," Brakes said. "I want to hear what Mr. Oakes has to say without any interruptions."

They drove for a while in silence, leaving the bustling streets of Norwich behind. Vera navigated the winding roads until they reached a secluded clearing near the edge of town. The trees surrounding the area provided enough cover from prying eyes, but the spot was still open enough that Brakes wouldn't feel trapped if things turned sour.

Brakes turned in his seat to face Peter. "Alright, talk. Start with why you were following the Marsh family, and what you know about John Marsh's murder."

Peter's eyes scanned the area before he finally focused on Brakes. "I worked for John Marsh," he admitted, his voice barely above a whisper. "I was one of his... runners, you could say."

"Smuggling?" Brakes pressed, though he already knew the answer.

Peter nodded, his hands fidgeting in his lap. "I never got involved in the bigger deals, just running packages. But I heard things. Saw things. John Marsh was into something deeper than smuggling. Something more dangerous."

"What kind of dangerous?" Brakes asked, narrowing his eyes. "If you're going to keep dancing around the truth, you can get out right now."

Peter flinched at the sharpness in Brakes' voice. "It's... it's weapons," he said, his voice barely a whisper now. "At first, it was just supplies. But a few months ago, John started dealing in arms—military-grade stuff. I think that's why he was killed. Someone wanted his operation, and they weren't going to ask nicely."

Brakes frowned. Weapon's smuggling wasn't entirely out of the realm of possibility—Norwich had a heavy military presence, and with the war going on, weapons were a valuable commodity. But John Marsh hadn't seemed like the type to get in over his head with something so risky.

"And you think you're next because you worked for him?" Brakes asked.

Peter shook his head frantically. "No, not just that. I know something. Something about the night he died. I wasn't there, but I know who was."

Brakes leaned forward, his voice dropping to a menacing whisper. "Then spit it out, man. Who killed John Marsh?"

Peter's face paled even further, and he looked like he might be sick. "It wasn't just one person," he said, his voice trembling. "It was a setup. I—I saw them. Three men, all of them wearing military uniforms. They weren't British soldiers. American, I think. I recognised one of them from their American uniform—he's been hanging around town for weeks now. He stands out like a sore thumb because the uniform he is wearing is so baggy, it's like he got dressed in the dark and picked up the wrong clothes."

Brakes' thoughts snapped back to the young man on the motorcycle, the one with the ill-fitting uniform.

"Vera, do you remember that rider we followed earlier?" Brakes asked slowly. "The one wearing the wrong uniform?"

Vera nodded. "You think he's one of them?"

Brakes turned back to Peter, his eyes narrowing. "Was he one of the men you saw?"

Peter hesitated, then nodded quickly. "Yes, I think so. A young man with an ill-fitting uniform, that sounds like him. He delivers packages on an American motorcycle, just like I used to. But now, he's moving more than just stolen goods."

Brakes sat back, his mind churning with the new information. He turned to Vera.

"We need to find that rider."

Vera gave a determined nod and turned the key in the ignition. As the car rumbled to life, Brakes cast one last glance at Peter, still pale and shaken in the back seat.

"You'd better not be lying, Oakes," he warned. "Because if you are, you're in a lot more trouble than you think."

Peter just swallowed and looked out of the window, his face now set in grim resignation as the car sped back toward Norwich.

Vera dropped Brakes and Oakes off at his house, and he instructed her to pick him up in the morning to take him to the Marsh estate. The moment he stepped out of the car and onto his doorstep, Brakes felt the familiar pull of his garage.

After emptying his bag and grabbing a quick lunch, Brakes told Oakes to stay in the house. "You will be safe here," Brakes promised him, and headed straight to for the garage.

The garage was his sanctuary, a place where he could unwind. The smell of grease, oil, and petrol instantly calmed his racing mind. The tension from the past few days began to melt away as he set to work, stripping the handlebars, front wheel and forks off one of his spare motorcycles. He took his time cleaning and polishing each part. His wrist, though much stronger now, still twinged with pain whenever he exerted too much pressure, a sharp reminder that it wasn't fully healed.

But Brakes wasn't one to listen to pain for long. He worked methodically, letting the motions of tinkering with the bike help him think.

John Marsh, his smuggling operation, the missing leg, the mysterious twin brother—everything felt connected, though the thread tying them together remained elusive.

CHAPTER NINE

The next morning broke with a grey sky hanging low over Norwich, the kind of oppressive clouds that promised rain. Brakes stood by his window, sipping his tea and staring out at the empty street, his mind already racing with thoughts about the case. Peter Oakes' confession from the day before had left him with more questions than answers, but it was a lead—one he intended to chase.

The memory of the young motorcyclist in the ill-fitting uniform nagged at him like a splinter he couldn't pull out. Could that rider be one of the Americans Peter had seen the night of John Marsh's murder? It seemed too much of a coincidence, and Brakes didn't believe in coincidences. He'd have to track the lad down and figure out who he was working for. But first, he needed to confront the Marsh family again. If John had been involved in arms smuggling, it was likely that someone in his family knew about it or at least suspected something.

Brakes glanced over at the clock. Vera would be arriving soon to take him back to the Marsh estate. He could feel the unease that always came before a difficult interrogation.

Ann Marsh, although she seemed completely broken by her brother's death at first, had a layer to her that appeared impenetrable. But Brakes had seen enough to know she wasn't telling him everything. It was time to press her further.

Just as Brakes placed his teacup in the sink, a knock came at the door. He opened it to find Vera standing there, her usual calm demeanour shadowed by something more serious today.

"Morning, sir," she said with a nod. "I called at the station prior to coming to pick you up and the sergeant gave me this note for you—it's another body."

Brakes frowned. "What? Did you read it? God damn it, Vera, how many times do I need to tell you? Some aspects of this case are not for your eyes or ears!" Snatching the paper angrily from her hand, Brakes read over it with a scowl. "Unless asked by me, I am ordering you to keep your nose out of this. The hovering close by and listening at doors, reading my paperwork—it has got to stop."

"Yes, sir." Vera replied, the corner of her lip twitching upwards in amusement. "So, I guess you don't want to know what the sergeant told me, then?"

Brakes' annoyance flared. "Honestly, talking to you is like trying to push water uphill with a cullender," he hissed, before asking, "Well? What did he say, then?"

"Dock workers found him early this morning when they were loading up a shipment. The uniformed officers think it's Peter Oakes," Vera replied, and Brakes' eyebrows shot up at the sound of Oakes' name.

"But it can't be. He is upstairs in bed. That's where I left him last night," Brakes replied before he sped upstairs to check Oakes' room.

Knocking on the door, Brakes called for Oakes. There was no answer, so after a moment, Brakes finally opened the door, only to find that the bed had not been touched all night. Slamming his good hand against the door frame, Brakes cursed loudly. "Damn it!"

Peter Oakes had known too much, and now he was dead. It was clear that someone was trying to tie up loose ends.

The docks were bustling with activity when they arrived. Despite the overcast sky, the workers moved with their usual efficiency, loading crates onto trucks and ships bound for the continent. War had changed the landscape of the city, and the docks had become a vital hub of activity. Brakes had always found the place chaotic, but today there was a stillness in the air.

Arriving at the docks, Vera parked as close as she could get. Uniformed officers guided Brakes to the scene, which was down an alley behind one of the large warehouses. The alley was damp, puddles of murky water dotting the ground. Brakes stepped carefully as he approached the body, now covered with a thick white sheet. The constable lifted the cover just enough for Brakes to get a look.

Peter Oakes lay crumpled on the ground, his face pale and bloodied. His jacket had been torn, and there were deep bruises along his neck and jaw. Crouching down, Brakes examined the body with the practised eye of a seasoned detective. It didn't take long to spot the cause of death—there were ligature marks around Peter's throat. He had been strangled.

"Looks like whoever did this wanted to make sure he couldn't talk," Brakes muttered, more to himself than to Vera, who was standing a few feet behind him. She crossed her arms tightly over her chest.

"Poor bastard didn't stand a chance, did he? Think it was the same people he was running from?" Vera asked, her gaze flicking between the body and Brakes.

Brakes stood up, wiping his hands on a handkerchief before tucking it back into his coat pocket. "It has to be. Peter said he knew too much, and now he's dead. It's no coincidence; someone's cleaning house, making sure no one talks."

Vera nodded grimly. "What do we do, now?"

Brakes turned and looked down the length of the alley, his mind already working through the possibilities. "I need to find that rider. If Peter was telling the truth, that young man is involved, and I'll bet he's part of a larger network," he explained, returning his gaze to Vera. "But first, I need to speak with Ann and Rosie again."

"If John Marsh was into arms smuggling, then perhaps this is what Ann is holding back." Brakes thought to himself.

The drive to the Marsh estate was a quiet one. The weight of Peter Oakes' murder hung over Brakes like a dark cloud, and the implications of his death were hard to shake. Someone was playing a dangerous game, and Brakes had a feeling they were running out of time to get ahead of it.

When they arrived at the estate, the large iron gates were already open, as if the Marsh family had been expecting them. Brakes found that suspicious, but he didn't comment on it. Instead, he focused on the task ahead: Getting the truth from Ann and Rosie.

Ann greeted them at the door, her face calm and poised. She wore a simple yet elegant dress, her hair neatly pinned back, not a strand out of place. Behind her, Rosie stood awkwardly, her eyes darting nervously between Ann and detective Brakes.

"Inspector Brakes," Ann greeted him coolly. "I wasn't expecting a visit so soon. Has there been any progress in the investigation?"

Brakes gave a tight smile. "We've made some headway, yes. But there are a few more things I need to clarify, if you don't mind."

Ann stepped aside, allowing Brakes and Vera to enter the grand foyer of the estate. The house was as pristine as ever, the marble floors gleaming in the dim light filtering through the windows. Yet Brakes could feel a chill in the air, not just from the weather but from the atmosphere inside the house. Something was wrong here.

"We can speak in the drawing room," Ann said, leading them through the hallway. "Rosie, why don't you join us after you have made some tea?"

Rosie hesitated, clearly uncomfortable, but followed Ann's instruction. Brakes noticed how the young woman's hands trembled slightly as she clasped them in front of her. She was hiding something. They both were.

Once they were seated in the drawing room, Brakes wasted no time. "I'm going to be direct with you, Miss. Marsh," he began, his tone firm. "We've discovered that your brother, John, was involved in more than just smuggling supplies—he was dealing in weapons. Dangerous ones."

Ann's expression barely changed, though her eyes darkened slightly. "I'm not sure what you're implying, Inspector."

Brakes leaned forward. "I'm not implying anything—I'm stating a fact. Your brother was murdered because of the business he was involved in, and I believe someone in this house knows more than they're letting on."

Rosie arrived just in time to hear Brakes' revelation, clutching a large tray of tea. Slowly, she placed it down on the coffee table.

Ann's jaw tightened at the accusation, but she remained silent. It was Rosie who spoke up, her voice barely audible. "I didn't know. I swear, I didn't know what John was doing."

Brakes shifted his gaze to Rosie, watching her carefully. "But you knew something, didn't you? Maybe not the full extent of his dealings, but you knew enough to be scared."

Rosie's hands trembled more visibly now. "I—I heard him talking to someone. A man. They were arguing about money, about shipments. I didn't understand most of it, but I knew it was something dangerous."

Brakes nodded. "And this man—did you ever see him?"

Rosie swallowed hard, glancing nervously towards Ann who shot her a warning look, but Rosie pressed on. "Once. I saw him in the garden late at night. He was wearing a military uniform, but it didn't look right. It was too big for him, and he didn't act like a soldier. He looked like he was trying to hide."

Brakes' heart quickened. The rider. It had to be him.

"Did you get a good look at him? Could you describe him?" he asked, perhaps too eagerly. Rosie bit her lip, her eyes welling up with tears.

"I don't remember much. He was young, with dark hair. But there was something else." She swallowed and took a deep breath, her body overcome by tremors. "He had a large scar on his face. You can't miss it."

Brakes' mind raced. The young man they had been following wasn't just some errand boy—he was involved in the arms smuggling ring, he had to be. Brakes stood up abruptly, turning to Vera. "I need to find that rider. *Now*."

Ann stood as well, her face a mask of control, but Brakes could see the tension behind her eyes. "Inspector, I assure you, I had no knowledge of John's illegal activities. We are just as much victims in this as anyone else."

Brakes gave her a hard look. "We'll see about that, Miss Marsh. But for now, we're going to find the men who killed your brother," he said and without another word, he and Vera left the room.

As they headed out of the house and back to the car, Brakes thought about Miss Marsh's newfound cold demeanour. It had not passed his notice, and the way she seemed to warn Rosie from revealing too much, even without words, reminded him to keep a close eye on them both.

As Brakes and Vera sped away from the Marsh estate, the cold truth of Peter Oakes' murder lingered in the back of Brakes' mind, and Rosie's description of the young rider with the ill-fitting uniform and scar was a tantalising lead. They had been close to catching him once before.

Vera's hands were steady on the wheel, but Brakes could sense her anxiety. She broke the silence first.

"So, where do we start? He could be anywhere by now, especially if he knows we're onto him."

Brakes rubbed his temples, thinking. "He's been spotted in town before. He must be staying nearby, maybe using one of the abandoned warehouses down by the docks." Brakes sighed and shook his head. "If he's involved in the smuggling, he'll need a place to stash goods."

Vera nodded. "And it's not just weapons he could be moving. Petrol, food rations, anything black-market related—those docks are crawling with opportunities."

"Really, Vera? And just how would you know that?" Asked Brakes.

"I grew up in Norwich. since war broke out, everyone in this town, in fact in the whole country, knows someone who knows someone THAT can get you things, for the right price. it's a common thing." She explained calmly, and Brakes could only nod in agreement.

Vera accelerated, and the engine roared as they headed back toward the docks where Peter Oakes had been found dead.

The docks were a maze of narrow streets and alleys, with abandoned warehouses lining the waterfront. Of course, there was no need to search the buildings nearby; they had already been searched when Oakes' body was found. It was the perfect place for illegal operations to go unnoticed, especially under the cover of war.

The grey sky above darkened, and the first drops of rain began to fall as they reached the waterfront district. The atmosphere was thick with the smell of sea salt and fish, mingling with the oily scent of machinery from the nearby ships. Dock workers moved in and out of the warehouses, but their activity seemed subdued, as if the recent discovery of a body had put everyone on edge.

Brakes and Vera parked the car near the alley where Peter Oakes had been found, but Brakes had no intention of investigating the crime scene again; something told him that there was more to the docklands than Oakes' final resting place.

"We'll split up, if you're okay with that, Vera," Brakes said, pulling his collar up to shield himself from the rain. "You take the east side, check the smaller warehouses. I'll take the west."

"I'll keep an eye out for any sign of the motorcycle," Vera said with a nod.

"No heroics, Vera," Brakes warned. "If you find anything, then come and get me, okay?"

They parted ways, and Brakes strode through the wet streets, his shoes splashing in the puddles that were forming in the cracks of the uneven cobblestone. He passed rows of warehouses, many of which had been abandoned since the war had shifted the cities priorities. The doors of some were padlocked, but others hung open, inviting anyone willing to risk whatever illicit activity lay inside.

The wind picked up, sending a chill through his coat, and Brakes' mind wandered back to the Marsh family. Ann's calm demeanour had cracked slightly during their last conversation, and Rosie's nervousness was impossible to ignore. There was more to the Marsh's than met the eye, but right now, the young rider was their best lead. If he could find the man, maybe it would all fall into place.

Brakes approached a larger warehouse at the edge of the docks. The windows were broken, and the building's once-bright paint had faded to a dull, peeling grey. Something about it felt right. He pulled out his flashlight, clicking it on as he stepped through the broken door. Inside, the space was vast and mostly empty, save for a few crates stacked near the walls. His footsteps echoed loudly in the stillness.

He swept the light across the room, stopping at a patch of floor near the back where the dirt had been disturbed recently. A faint line of tire tracks led toward a side door—*motorcycle tracks.*

Brakes' heart quickened. He followed the tracks through the side door, stepping into a narrow passageway that led toward a back alley. Just as he was about to step out into the open, he froze.

Close by, the sound of an engine revved.

Brakes pressed himself against the wall, peering around the corner. There, in the alley, was the motorcycle, and next to it stood the rider, fumbling with something in his saddlebag. His back was to Brakes, but the ill-fitting uniform gave him away.

Brakes' pulse raced. He had found him.

Steeling himself, Brakes crept forward, careful not to make a sound. The rider was distracted, clearly in a hurry to leave. Brakes was just a few steps away when a loud *clang* echoed through the alley—the sound of a metal bin being knocked over in the distance.

The rider spun around, and before Brakes could reach for his weapon, the young man jumped on his motorcycle, kicking it into life.

"Stop!" Brakes cried, but it was too late.

The motorcycle roared to life, its rear tire producing a rooster tail from the laying water on the cobblestones as the rider sped down the alley. Brakes cursed and sprinted after him, but the bike was already disappearing around the corner.

Out of breath, Brakes stopped, watching helplessly as the rider vanished into the maze of streets. He kicked the wall in frustration—he had been so close, and now the trail was slipping away again.

Suddenly, the sound of another engine reached his ears—Vera's car. She must have heard the commotion. A moment later, the car screeched around the corner, pulling up beside Brakes.

"Get in!" Vera yelled.

Brakes didn't hesitate. He threw open the passenger door and jumped in, and Vera hit the accelerator, the tires skidding as they took off in the direction the rider had fled.

"He's fast, but he won't be able to manoeuvre as well as we can due to the wet roads and narrow streets," Brakes said, scanning the road ahead for any sign of the rider.

Vera nodded, her face set with determination. "I'll stay on him. He won't get away this time."

They tore through the dockside streets, the rain coming down harder now, making the roads slick and dangerous. Brakes kept his eyes peeled for the flash of the motorcycle's taillights, but the winding streets made it difficult to track their quarry.

Finally, as they rounded a corner, Brakes spotted the rider up ahead, weaving through the traffic as he tried to lose them. Vera gritted her teeth, swerving to avoid a cart full of fish being pushed across the road.

"There!" Brakes pointed.

The rider had made a sharp turn into a narrow alleyway, barely wide enough for the car to follow. Vera didn't hesitate, turning the wheel sharply and sending the car screeching into the alley after him. The walls seemed to close in around them, and Brakes could hear the sound of the car's tires scraping against the brick.

But Vera was relentless. She kept the car steady, inching closer to the rider with each passing second.

"We're going to run out of room," Brakes said, eyes locked on the figure ahead.

"There's only one way out, straight ahead," replied a determined Vera.

Sure enough, the alleyway ended in a dead end. The rider skidded to a stop. His eyes grew wide with panic once the realisation had dawned on him that he was trapped.

Vera slammed on the brakes, bringing the car to a screeching halt just feet from the motorcycle. Brakes was out of the car in an instant, drawing his revolver and aiming it squarely at the rider.

"Don't move!" Brakes shouted, his voice ringing through the alley.

The rider froze, his hands gripping the handlebars of the motorcycle. Slowly, he raised them in surrender.

Brakes approached cautiously, keeping his weapon trained on the young man. Up close, he could see the fear in the rider's eyes, but there was something else too—defiance.

"You've got nowhere to go," Brakes said, his voice cold. "Now, tell me—who are you, and who are you working for?"

The rider didn't answer, his jaw clenched tightly as he stared back at Brakes.

"I'm not asking again," Brakes warned, stepping closer. Keeping his weapon trained on the lad, Brakes instructed Vera to cuff their newest suspect. Once the cuffs were secure, Brakes led him to the car, placed him on the backseat, shut the door, and entered the car on the passenger side.

"Right, you're in a lot of trouble, so you better start talking, and fast," Brakes growled, his gun still poised squarely on the lad. For a moment, the rider seemed to waver, his eyes darting around as if searching for a way out. Only, there was none.

Finally, after a moment of contemplation, he spoke, his voice low and raspy. "You have no idea what you're getting into, Inspector."

Brakes' grip tightened on his revolver. "Try me."

The rider smirked, but there was no humour in it. "It's too late. You can't stop it now."

Before Brakes could react, the rider spoke again. "There's something for you inside my jacket," he said, clearly amused by the situation. "I would give it to you myself, but my hands are tied, you see." He jostled the handcuffs, as if to make a point.

Wary, Brakes reached over the seat and pulled open the rider's jacket. There, he could see the outline of a hidden pocket. The rider didn't move as Brakes reached in and pulled out something small and metallic. When he finally brought it close to his face, Brakes' heart raced. He had thought the lad would be hiding a weapon, but what Brakes was holding wasn't a gun—it was a key.

"A warehouse," the rider said, his voice almost mocking. "It's all there. Everything you're looking for."

Brakes frowned, lowering his revolver slightly. "What warehouse?"

The rider's smirk widened. "Why should I tell you anymore? What's in it for me?"

"Look, stop messing around," Brakes growled unsympathetically, his thread of patience ready to snap. "I already have you bang to rights on several charges. Don't add obstruction to the list."

The rider rolled his eyes. "Okay, you can't blame a guy for trying," he sighed. "You need to go to Dock 17, warehouse 4. You'll find your answers there."

Brakes exchanged a quick glance with Vera, who had been silently watching the exchange from the driver's seat. She gave him a nod, her expression grim. Wirth his heart pounding in his chest, Brakes turned back to the rider. Dock 17. It was a lead.

But something about the rider's smirk made Brakes uneasy. There was more to this than he was letting on, and whatever waited for them at Dock 17, Brakes had a feeling it wouldn't be easy to walk away from.

CHAPTER TEN

The sun was barely visible through the clouds, but at least it had stopped raining as Brakes and Vera drove toward Dock 17. The key from the mysterious rider, who still hadn't given his name, weighed heavily in Brakes' pocket. The narrow streets were slick with rainwater, the buildings looming in the early evening light like silent witnesses to the secrets hidden within them.

Vera's voice broke through the quiet, low and steady. "This could be a trap, you know."

Brakes didn't respond right away, his mind replaying his conversation with the lad. The man's smirk, his cryptic words, the strange key—it all felt wrong. Yet, it was their only lead. With Peter Oakes dead, and the trail around John Marsh's murder growing colder by the day, they couldn't afford to ignore it.

From beside him, the rider grinned.

"I know," Brakes said, his gaze fixed on the road ahead. "But we're out of options. Whatever's waiting for us at Dock 17, it's connected to Marsh, to Oakes—to all of it."

Vera nodded, but didn't seem comforted. "Let's just be smart about this. No heroics, okay, sir? We should call the station and get more officers here." She adjusted her grip on the steering wheel, her knuckles white. Brakes gave her a tight smile.

"Wouldn't dream of it," he said. "Of course, you're right, but if we wait for them, we might miss our quarry. And we don't want to do that, now, do we, Vera?"

"No, sir," Vera replied, almost begrudgingly. "I suppose not."

As they approached Dock 17, the skyline of abandoned warehouses rose up around them, their empty windows dark and foreboding. The dock itself was eerily quiet, save for the occasional squawk of a seagull or the distant creak of ropes from the nearby ships moored in the harbour. The area seemed deserted, the perfect place for illicit dealings and hidden transactions.

Vera pulled the car into the shadow of a large, rusting crane and killed the engine. They sat in silence for a moment, bracing themselves.

"You ready?" Brakes asked, his hand resting on the door handle. Vera nodded, her expression set.

"Let's get this over with. But first, let's secure this idiot on the back seat," Vera said, turning in her seat. She glared at the rider, who simply grinned back, clearly amused by the situation. "We don't want him to abscond whilst we're away from the car, now, do we, sir?"

"Great idea, Vera. I'll do it."

Brakes set to securing their prisoner to the bottom of the seat. Once he was done, both he and Vera stepped out of the car, the sound of their boots on the damp cobblestone the only noise cutting through the stillness. Brakes led the way, the key clutched tightly in his hand as they approached the entrance to Warehouse 17. The door was old and heavy, the paint peeling and rust eating away at the metal hinges.

With a quick glance toward Vera, Brakes slipped the key into the padlock. It turned with a soft click.

"Stay close," Brakes muttered as he pushed the door open, pulling his weapon from its holster.

The inside of the warehouse was dark and cavernous, the faint smell of dampness hanging in the air. Shafts of pale light filtered in through the high windows, casting eerie shadows on the concrete floor. Stacks of crates lined the walls, some marked with military insignias, others with faded shipping labels from overseas.

Brakes and Vera moved cautiously, their footsteps echoing in the emptiness. There was something unsettling about the place—too quiet, too empty. Brakes could feel the hairs on the back of his neck beginning to prickle, as if standing to attention.

"I don't like this," Vera whispered, her hand resting on Brakes' shoulder.

Brakes didn't like it either. He scanned the room, looking for anything that seemed out of place, but everything seemed abandoned, forgotten. The crates looked as if they had been untouched for years, covered in dust, and there were no signs of recent activity.

"This can't be it," Vera said, frustration creeping into her voice. "Where's the smuggling operation? Where's the proof?"

Brakes' brow furrowed as he moved deeper into the warehouse, his eyes drawn to a cluster of crates in the far corner. Something about the arrangement of them seemed off—too deliberate, too organised in contrast to the disarray of the rest of the place.

He gestured for Vera to follow him, and they approached the crates. Brakes knelt down, running his fingers along the edges of one. It wasn't sealed like the others, and as he pried the lid open, the contents inside took him by surprise.

Guns!

Dozens of them, stacked neatly in rows. Rifles, pistols, and even a few submachine guns—all in pristine condition. These were fresh, likely stolen from military stockpiles, and being prepared for distribution.

"Smuggling weapons," Vera breathed, her eyes wide.

Brakes nodded and his jaw tightened. "This is what Oakes stumbled onto, and what Marsh might have been involved in. But who's running it?"

Before Vera could respond, the sound of footsteps echoed from somewhere deep within the warehouse. Brakes and Vera exchanged a look, and he signalled for her to take cover behind the crates with him.

The footsteps grew louder, more deliberate, and soon a small group of figures emerged from the shadows at the far end of the warehouse. Brakes squinted, trying to make out their faces, but the dim light made it difficult.

Suddenly, a familiar voice cut through the silence.

"Well, well. I wasn't expecting company."

Brakes' blood ran cold. He knew that voice. Stepping into the light, flanked by two burly men, was none other than...

"*Ann?*"

Vera's voice came out as a soft gasp. At the sound of her name, Ann smiled, a cold, calculating thing that sent a chill down Brakes' spine.

"Inspector Brakes. Always sticking your nose where it doesn't belong, I see," she stated coolly, her gaze narrowing down at Brakes' hunched figure. He stood slowly, keeping his gun trained on her.

"You're behind all this, Ann?" Brakes hissed accusingly. Ann's smile widened. "The smuggling, Oakes' and John's murder... everything?"

Ann took a few steps closer, her hands casually resting in the pockets of her elegant coat. She seemed entirely unfazed by the gun pointed at her.

"I'm not behind *everything*," she said, her voice dripping with mock innocence. "But I've had my part to play. As for Peter Oakes... well, he should've known better than to cross the wrong people."

Brakes felt a surge of anger. "So, you had him killed? Because he knew too much?"

Ann shrugged. Her eyes were cold. "He was a loose end. And I don't like loose ends."

Vera stepped forward, her face pale. "But why, Ann? Why smuggle weapons? What does any of this have to do with your brother's murder?"

Ann's expression darkened. "John wasn't supposed to get involved. He was reckless, always trying to prove something." She sounded bitter, but her words were laced with remorse. "When he found out what I was doing, he tried to stop me—threatened to go to the police. So, I had to make a choice."

Brakes' heart sank. It all made sense now—John Marsh had discovered his sister's involvement in the smuggling ring and had tried to put an end to it.

"So, you had him killed, too," Brakes said, his voice stern.

Ann's smile faded, replaced by a cold-glare. "John was family. I didn't want to hurt him, but business is business, Inspector, and in this world, you either adapt, or you get left behind."

Before Brakes could respond, one of the men standing behind Ann raised a gun of his own, pointing it directly at him.

"Drop the weapon, Inspector," the man growled.

Brakes' grip on his revolver tightened, but he knew he was outnumbered. Reluctantly, Brakes lowered his weapon and placed it on the floor. Ann's smile returned, but this time, it was triumphant.

"Smart choice, Inspector," Ann said, her tone mocking. Brakes could only stare back at her calmly, but beneath his facade, fury boiled. He had been outmanoeuvred.

Ann turned back to her men. "Tie them up. We'll deal with them later."

The ropes bit into Brakes' wrists as one of Ann's goons yanked them tight, binding him to a steel support beam in the centre of the warehouse. Vera was tied to the next beam, her face twisted with frustration. The two thugs had worked quickly, their hands rough and experienced.

Ann watched from a distance with her arms crossed.

Brakes could feel the cold, damp air settle in around him, seeping into his skin. His eyes darted around the warehouse, searching for a way out, before turning back to the men to see if he could find any weakness in them, or their situation.

There was nothing. They were stuck; in a vain attempt to uncover the truth, Brakes had stumbled onto something far bigger than he had ever imagined, and now both he and Vera were caught in the middle of it.

And if they didn't find a way out soon, it was clear that neither of them would live to see another day.

"So, what happens next, Ann?" Brakes asked, trying to keep his voice even. "You kill us? Stage another accident? You think that'll cover this up?"

Ann smiled, cold and unfeeling. "Oh, Brakes; always the dramatist. I don't have to stage anything." Sighing, she sauntered over, her heels clicking on the concrete floor. She stood in front of Brakes, her face a mask of calm, yet her eyes betrayed her. As Ann looked down at Brakes, he could see her amusement over the situation, as well as the disdain that she held for him. Brakes' jaw clenched.

"And when Vera and I turn up dead, what then? People talk, Ann. They'll dig. They always dig, more so my fellow policemen," he said, a clear warning behind his words. For a moment, Brakes could see Ann's mask slip as her smirk faltered, worry flickering into her eyes before her gaze hardened again.

"Perhaps. But by then, I'll be long gone, and so will the weapons," she explained, and leaned in closer until her perfume felt cloying against the cool air. "I know people in high places, Brakes. People who won't let some nosy Inspector get in their way."

She straightened, turning her attention to her henchmen. "Get them in the truck. We leave in an hour."

The thugs grunted in acknowledgment, one of them moving toward the far end of the warehouse where an old military truck was parked. Brakes could hear the engine rumble to life, its low growl vibrating through the floor. Without a second glance, Ann disappeared behind a stack of crates, leaving Brakes and Vera to be watched by her remaining beady-eyed henchman.

Vera leaned her head back against the beam, closing her eyes. "This is a fine mess," she muttered under her breath.

Brakes pulled against the ropes, testing their strength. His wrists were beginning to feel raw, but he wasn't going to give up that easily. "We'll get out of this," he said, more to himself than to Vera. Opening one eye, Vera speared him with a sidelong glance.

"You got a plan, sir? Because if you do, now's the time."

Brakes' eyes darted around the warehouse again, searching for anything that could give them an edge. His gaze fell on a pile of loose metal rods scattered near the base of one of the beams. They were out of reach, but if he could just get his hands free…

As he twisted his hands against his binds, Brakes felt the rope catch onto something behind him. Feeling around with his fingers, he felt a sharp prick against his skin—there, sticking out of the beam he had been tied to, was a small splinter of metal, its edge sharp. This was it, Brakes realised—*this* was how he was going to get out.

The sound of footsteps echoed as the goon made his way towards Brakes and Vera. Brakes immediately slumped against the beam, and the thug chuckled.

"Giving up already, Inspector? I thought you'd be tougher than that."

Brakes didn't respond, waiting for the man to get closer. Beside him, Vera began to shift as the thug moved within arm's reach and crouched down to check the ropes around Brakes' ankles. That was the opening Brakes needed, and with a sudden burst of energy, he kicked out with both feet, knocking the man off balance.

The thug fell back with a grunt, hitting the floor hard. Before the thug could react, Brakes twisted his bound hands, managing to catch the edge of the metal splinter. It took a few sharp tugs, but Brakes was able to quickly cut himself free and practically threw himself across the warehouse floor.

The thug let out what Brakes could only describe as a roar, and he turned to see the man getting ready to launch himself toward Brakes. Grabbing one of the metal rods, he struck the thug square in the face, sending him sprawling unconscious onto the concrete.

"I'll be damned," Vera gasped, her eyes growing wide. "Can you do that again? I missed most of it, sir. It was too fast."

Ignoring her question, Brakes moved to quickly untie his ankles, before moving onto Vera's binds. Once free, she began flexing her fingers and rolling her ankles.

"Next time, you could untie me a little faster, you know," she said playfully, wincing when she stretched out her arms. Brakes grinned.

"Noted."

Hearing the commotion, the remaining thug returned from the truck, his eyes growing wide as he took in the scene before him.

"Oi!" he cried, his face growing blotchy and red with anger. "They're loose!" And before Brakes or Vera could react, the man charged at them both, a thick length of pipe raised above his head. Brakes immediately ducked under the swing, the pipe whistling past his ear, and without hesitation he stepped forward, jabbing the metal rod into the thug's gut.

The man doubled over, dropping his pipe as he gasped for air. Vera, who had run to find a weapon, delivered the finishing blow, and slammed a crate lid down onto the thug's head. Breathing heavily, Brakes and Vera watched as the man finally crumpled to the ground, out cold.

Wiping his brow, Brakes stepped forward and bent down to retrieve his revolver. He turned back to Vera. "Well, that wasn't too bad."

Vera nodded, catching her breath. "We need to move quickly, though. Ann's still here, and she'll have reinforcements."

Brakes glanced toward the truck. "We're going to use her own escape plan against her."

Vera raised an eyebrow. "You mean the truck?"

"Exactly." Brakes grabbed the keys from the unconscious thug and tossed them to Vera. "You drive—I'll handle Ann."

They climbed into the truck, with Brakes hanging out of the cab as Vera gripped the wheel, a determined glint in her eyes while she manoeuvred the truck around the warehouse. Ann was still somewhere inside, likely organising her next move, but Brakes couldn't let her get away with it.

The warehouse was a maze of crates and machinery, but they persevered until Brakes finally spotted Ann near the rear of the building, speaking hurriedly with another figure—an older man, tall and distinguished, his greying hair slicked back.

"Stop the truck and turn off the engine, and don't leave the vehicle," Brakes instructed. Vera did as she was asked, and Brakes quietly stepped out of the truck and hid behind a stack of crates to watch the exchange. A moment later, he witnessed the man handing a thick envelope to Ann. Even from afar, Brakes could see the greed that clouded Ann's gaze before she tucked the envelope into her coat.

"Was this it?" Brakes wondered. Was this the contract that had funded the entire operation?

Stepping out of the shadows, Brakes aimed his revolver directly at Ann. "This ends now," he yelled, his voice loud and clear. Ann turned to face him, surprise passing over her face. Then she narrowed her eyes.

"You're persistent, I'll give you that," Ann sneered.

"Who the hell are you?" The older man spat out, looking towards Brakes with a dark expression. Cocking his gun, Brakes looked towards the stranger and smiled.

"Inspector Brakes," he replied evenly. "And you're under arrest."

Ann laughed, a sharp, bitter sound. "You really think you can stop this, Brakes? You have no idea how deep this goes."

Brakes took a step forward, his grip steady on the gun. "I know enough, and I'm not letting you walk away from this."

Before Ann could respond, the older man reached inside his coat, and Brakes tensed. But before the man could draw whatever weapon he was going for, the sound of screeching tires echoed throughout the warehouse.

Ann and her accomplish looked towards the noise, clearly startled, as Vera drove the truck straight toward them, stopping just inches from Ann and her accomplice.

Ann's eyes widened in surprise, but before she could react, Brakes dashed forward and grabbed her by the arm, twisting it behind her back and pinning her against the crates.

"I told you," Brakes said quietly. "It's over."

Ann struggled, but Brakes held her firm. The older man, thinking this was his chance, started to back away. Vera took that moment to step out of the truck, holding a revolver she had taken from one of the thugs, and trained it on the man. Immediately, he froze in his tracks.

"Don't even think about it," she warned. The man raised his hands slowly, his face a mask of fury.

"You're making a mistake, Inspector," he hissed, his gaze sliding over to Brakes. "You're meddling in things you don't understand."

Brakes ignored him, focusing on Ann. "I'll be sure to explain everything to the judge. Maybe they'll go easy on you."

"You don't know what you're doing, Brakes," Ann snapped with a glare, though it seemed as if her cold demeanour was finally cracking. "This operation is bigger than me, bigger than all of us. You're just a pawn."

Brakes tightened his grip. "Maybe. But pawns can still take down a queen."

CHAPTER ELEVEN

The sun was just rising over Norwich, casting long shadows across the empty streets as Brakes and Vera sat in silence outside the station. They had just handed Ann Marsh and her accomplices over to the custody sergeant with charges for smuggling, treason, kidnapping, attacking a police officer... the list seemed endless.

The events of the past few days gnawed at Brakes. The close calls, an unravelling conspiracy—it all came down on him like an iron anchor. And then there were Ann's parting words about him being a pawn, and how the operation went deeper than he could imagine.

As he looked out over the city, still waking up to another day, he knew they were far from finished.

"You're thinking about Marsh's murder, aren't you?" Vera asked, shattering the quiet that had fallen between them.

Brakes nodded slowly, his gaze distant. "It's all connected. Ann might have been running the smuggling operation, but there's something bigger going on. Marsh's murder was a message—a warning. It just doesn't feel finished."

Vera leaned back in the driver's seat, her fingers tapping lightly on the wheel. "Do you think someone higher up ordered it? Maybe someone in the government?"

"Maybe. The man we picked up with her—he's no small fry. He was calm, too calm for someone in handcuffs. And he mentioned I was 'meddling in things I didn't understand.'" Brakes turned to face Vera, his brow furrowing. "He's right. There's more to this than just a black-market operation."

"You think this goes higher than Ann?"

"I'd bet my badge on it."

Vera sighed, her gaze dropping to the steering wheel. "So, where do we start?"

Brakes shifted uncomfortably, rolling his sore wrists. The events of the night were catching up to him, his body reminding him of the struggle.

"We start with John Marsh. We still don't know why he was killed, or who really did it." Brakes grimaced. "Ann couldn't have pulled it off on her own—she might've hired someone, or she could be covering for someone else. Either way, we need to look deeper into the Marsh family. Someone's pulling the strings, and I intend to find out who."

Vera gave him a tired but determined nod. "Then let's get to it."

They stepped out of the truck, the early morning chill settling over them as they headed inside the station. The familiar scent of paper, ink, and stale coffee greeted them as they entered. Constables and detectives bustled about, most too engrossed in their own tasks to notice Brakes and Vera.

The desk sergeant, an older man with thinning hair, glanced up from his paperwork as they approached.

"Morning, Inspector. I heard you brought in Ann Marsh and a group of her lot last night. Quite the catch, eh?"

Brakes leaned on the counter, pitching his voice low. "Keep an eye on them, especially the older man. He's dangerous, and he's got connections."

The sergeant nodded, scribbling something on the paperwork in front of him. "Understood. I'll make sure they're well-guarded."

Brakes turned away. "Come on, Vera. We've got work to do."

The drive from the station to the Marsh estate was a quiet one. It seemed as if Vera's own thoughts were consumed by the past evening's events, which suited Brakes well. He could not deal with Vera's usual penchant for questions, not when he had so many to ask himself.

As Brakes and Vera pulled up the long driveway, the house loomed before them, its stone façade bathed in the pale light of the morning. The place felt different now—emptier, colder. The last time they had been here, they were searching for answers.

This time, Brakes intended to find them.

They were met at the door by an elderly woman. She seemed familiar somehow, yet Brakes just couldn't put his finger on it. Her face was impassive, but there was something in her eyes—a flicker of uncertainty. She nodded curtly.

"Inspector, Miss Vera. I wasn't expecting you."

Brakes didn't waste time with pleasantries. "What are you doing on this estate, in this house?"

The woman hesitated for a moment. "I was asked to watch over the place by the Marsh family, if anything were to happen to them," she replied.

"Then I will need your full name and address before we leave, madam. Okay?" he said, taking a step closer toward the doorway. The woman stood firm, however, her gaze unwavering.

"Certainly, Inspector. I will have that ready for you," the woman acquiesced, her tone pleasant enough. Nodding, Brakes stepped forward once again, practically toeing the threshold.

"Now, stand aside. Is Rosie at home?" asked Brakes as he entered the entrance hall, and the woman finally moved aside, her lips set into a grim line as she turned and called for Rosie. Minutes later, Rosie emerged and stepped slowly down the grand staircase.

"Inspector. How may I help you?" she asked, her voice small. As she came closer, Brakes could see how pale and drawn Rosie was, her eyes rimmed red. Clearly, losing her mistress had affected the young woman greatly.

"Good morning, Rosie. May I speak to you in private, please?" he asked. There was a short pause but, finally, Rosie nodded and gestured for them to follow her to the drawing room.

As they walked through the hallway, Vera looked around with wide eyes, surveying the grand interior. Brakes recalled that the last time she had come to the manor, she barely had any time to look around as they investigated Marsh's room. So, upon entering the drawing room, Vera's mouth formed into a small 'o' as she took in the antique furniture and heavy drapes.

A large oil painting of Ann Marsh's mother, Mrs. Beatrice Marsh, hung above the stone fireplace, her portrayal immortalised as she sat ramrod straight in a high-backed chair. Her gaze felt discerning as she watched over the three of them gathering in the lavish space.

Moving toward the fireplace, Rosie took the poker and stoked the fire, her expression guarded. Silence settled between the three of them as the flames crackled, no one daring to speak. Finally, without turning to face either Brakes or Vera, Rosie spoke.

"Inspector Brakes," Rosie said, her voice weak but steady. "Why are you here? Haven't you taken enough from this family already?"

She finally turned to look at them, the flicker of the flames highlighting her face. Brakes could see the remnants of tears on her cheeks. Stepping forward, Brakes cleared his throat.

"Rosie, we're here because we have arrested Ann for her involvement in John's death," he started, his tone firm but respectful. "Which, we now believe, is connected to a much larger conspiracy."

Rosie simply stared back at Brakes, her lips pressed into a thin line. She did not discredit his words, however, nor did she try and fight back. Brakes pressed on.

"She'll face justice, of course, but we need to know more. John's death—it wasn't just a random act of violence, or because he had uncovered what Ann was up to." He paused, gauging Rosie's reaction. Her eyes betrayed nothing, so Brakes continued. "Someone wanted him dead for a much deeper reason, and I think you know what that reason is."

Rosie hesitated. Finally, she put down the poker and moved away from the fireplace. Her hands began to tremble as she walked the length of the room, stopping at the window to look out of it.

"John... he was a good man on the surface, yes. But he was always involved in one thing or another."

She swallowed, shook her head, and sighed. "Illegal activities, I mean, and of course his drinking. But he was always small fry, searching. Looking for that big pay day. Once he got his teeth into something, though, he wouldn't let it go."

She took a shuddering breath and turned back to Brakes and Vera, her voice soft. "He didn't deserve what happened to him, not for a moment."

"I don't doubt that, but we've uncovered evidence that suggests John might have been involved in something dangerous—something that got him killed," Brakes explained brusquely. Rosie's eyes narrowed. "Ann was running a smuggling operation, and we believe John found out about it. Was that what led to his death?"

Rosie began to tremble, her gaze fierce. "You've got no right to come here and accuse this family of this. Ann wasn't involved in any smuggling. She—"

"Rosie," Brakes interrupted, his voice gentle but firm. "We caught her at the scene, surrounded by crates of guns, and accepting an envelope full of cash."

At his words, Rosie bit her lip, trying to keep her emotions from flashing across her face. She glared at them both and instead moved to take a seat across from Brakes and Vera. Taking a deep breath, Brakes continued.

"Rosie, if you know something—anything—that could help us, now is the time to speak up," he explained, his tone urgent. "John's death was no accident. We've seen how far Ann was willing to go to protect her operation. But I believe she wasn't acting alone."

For a long moment, the room was silent, the air heavy with unspoken words. Rosie's eyes fell to her lap, her hands twisting in the fabric of a nearby blanket. When she finally spoke, her voice was barely above a whisper.

"John, he… he found out something he wasn't supposed to. About Ann, yes, but also about others—powerful people. People who wouldn't hesitate to… to silence him."

Brakes felt a chill run down his spine. "Who, Rosie? Who was involved?"

Rosie shook her head slowly, tears welling in her eyes. "I don't know their names. Neither Ann nor John told me everything. But he was scared. I'd never seen him like that before." She sniffed, still shaking her head, and whispered, "He told me he was going to the police, but… but then…" Her voice broke, and she covered her face with her hands, her body wracked with sobs.

Brakes' heart pounded as he began to pace the room. This was it—the confirmation he had been searching for. John Marsh had been killed because he knew too much. Ann was just one piece of the puzzle, but there were others—people in positions of power who had orchestrated the murder to protect themselves.

As Brakes and Vera left the estate, the knowledge of what they had just uncovered settled in their minds. They had a lead, but the road ahead was dangerous—the people behind John's murder wouldn't stop at just two deaths to protect their secrets, especially now that Brakes and Vera knew too much.

Back at the station, Brakes sat at his desk, his thoughts clouded with questions and possibilities. Vera sat across from him, flipping through a newspaper, her brow furrowed in concentration.

Brakes nodded. "We need to tread carefully. If what everyone has said is true, we're dealing with powerful people—people who have the means to make us disappear, and without hesitation."

Vera tapped her pen against the table. "So, what's the next move?"

Brakes leaned back in his chair, staring up at the ceiling. "If in doubt, always follow the money. Someone was funding Ann's operation, and whoever it was, they're the key to unravelling this whole thing," he explained, turning his gaze to Vera. "As for you, Vera, you're not a police officer. It's best you keep out of this from now on, for your own safety."

"To hell with that, sir," Vera said sharply, the newspaper forgotten as she stared up at Brakes. "I started this with you, and if you don't mind, I want to see it through to the end, regardless of the consequences, sir."

Sighing, Brakes ran a hand over his face. "I have to report to the Chief," he said gruffly, and got up from his seat. "We'll talk about this later." And before Vera could respond, Brakes got up and left his desk.

The clock ticked on, the familiar hum of the station around him falling into the background as he made his way to the Chief's office. His mind ran through every piece of information, every conversation, and every clue they had gathered so far. Brakes now had his finger on the pulse of a conspiracy that he could barely comprehend, and John Marsh had found himself in the thick of it.

The Chief saw Brakes immediately, and after a thorough debrief, the Chief sat back in his chair and tapped his chin in thought.

"If we're going to follow the money, we'll need help," the Chief said, his gaze fixed on the ceiling. "Someone on the inside—someone who can trace financial records, hidden accounts. Things that aren't visible at first glance."

Brakes rubbed his temples. "You're right. We can't just walk into a bank and demand to see their ledgers. We need someone discreet, someone who knows their way around this kind of thing."

"Don't you have a friend in secret service, Brakes?" the Chief recalled. For a moment, he ruminated over his thoughts, and then his eyes brightened. "Richard Harris."

"Harris? The forensic accountant?" Brakes raised an eyebrow. "Last I heard, he was tied up with some corporate fraud case in London."

"I've worked with him before. If anyone can trace where the money's coming from, it's Harris." The Chief nodded; his decision was already made. "I'll give him a call."

Brakes could not help but notice the sudden change in his superior's mood as the Chief sat up, his lips almost curving into a smile. Brakes took this as his cue to leave and began making his way to the door as the Chief reached for his telephone. Brakes paused, his hand now poised over the door handle.

Clearing his throat, he turned back to the Chief. "And Vera, sir?"

With the telephone pressed to his ear, the Chief stared at Brakes for a long moment. "Keep her with you for now, Brakes," he said, his tone final. "Two heads are better than one, after all."

Nodding, Brakes turned to leave again, but the Chief's next words cut through him, just loud enough for Brakes to hear.

"Perhaps having her there will keep you out of trouble, for now."

Brakes left abruptly after that, immediately returning to his desk where Vera sat, waiting for him. Briefly, he went over what the Chief had said regarding their next move.

Vera listened attentively, but there was still a lingering doubt in her eyes. "Sir, do you think it's really about money. Couldn't it just be about power—keeping control of their operations?"

Brakes leaned forward, resting his elbows on the desk. "It's always about money, Vera. Especially when you're talking about smuggling on this scale. The people behind this aren't just street thugs—they're well-connected. They've got resources, and they're not afraid to use them."

She nodded, and Brakes paused for a moment. Vera looked up at him almost expectantly, waiting for what he had to say next. Shifting his gaze to the desk, Brakes started shuffling through papers, delaying the inevitable. Finally, he looked back up at Vera and bit the bullet.

"Now, I have spoken to the Chief regarding yourself, and he has suggested that you can continue to help on this case," he began reluctantly, and immediately, Vera's eyes gleamed with excitement.

"Just tell me what to do, sir," Vera exclaimed happily, her body practically vibrating with anticipation. Holding a hand up, Brakes quieted her. He was already beginning to regret this.

"There will be no more getting in the middle of dangerous situations," he continued sternly. Vera's smile widened. "You are my driver, first and foremost. You are *not* my partner. Do you understand?"

"Yes, sir," she replied, nodding eagerly. "Anything that will help you and prevent me being transferred back to my old unit."

Brakes sighed. "Just try to stay out of trouble, Vera," he said tiredly, the weariness of the past few days finally creeping into his bones. Every step forward felt like walking into quicksand—progressive but dangerous, sinking deeper with each revelation.

Standing from his chair, Brakes stretched and stared down at Vera. "It's been a long day. I think it's time to go home. Fetch the car, if you will"

The rest of the evening passed without issue, and the next morning, Vera picked Brakes up from his home and took him to the station. Once they arrived at his desk, however, they were greeted by a visitor.

"Well, well," the man said, his chuckle low upon seeing Brakes. "It's been a while."

Brakes' attention spiked at the familiar voice, before a tired smile broke out on his lips at seeing his old friend.

"Harris. How are you, old chap?" he said, holding out his hand for a firm shake. "I assume the Chief called? I must say, you have arrived earlier than expected."

Harris nodded, his expression passive. "Indeed. This is not a social call, of course; something about a case, I hear?" Then, he glanced briefly at Vera and offered her a curt nod in greeting, which she returned.

"Yes," Brakes murmured, before turning to Vera. "Vera, I have an important matter to attend to. Please, go fuel up the car and have a cup of tea. I will call for you soon."

At his dismissal, Vera looked visibly displeased but made no argument. With a small nod, she removed herself from the station quickly, leaving both Brakes and Harris alone at Brakes' desk. Sinking into his chair, Brakes waved a hand towards the seat across from him, and Harris sat down.

"So, what has the Chief told you?" Brakes asked, leaning back in his chair.

"Enough to intrigue me." Harris smiled, folding his hands on top of the desk. "Quite the mess you've got yourself into here, Brakes. Smuggling, black-market operations, and, of course, some suspicious financial transactions that you cannot quite trace. Correct?"

Brakes nodded. "Yes," he said, sighing deeply. "And I need someone with your expertise to help us follow the money."

"Well, it certainly sounds far more exciting than the usual fraud cases I follow," Harris said, chuckling again. "But you know me—I like a challenge. Just how deep does this all go, exactly?"

"Deep enough that two people have been murdered, all because they knew too much." Brakes offered, and Harris let out a low whistle.

"Alright," he agreed, leaning back in his chair. "I'll need details, records. Anything you've got."

Brakes continued to fill Harris in on the essentials, and Harris had informed him that, after the Chief's call the afternoon before, he had already prepared the tools needed to begin unravelling the financial side of the operation, and would bring them to the station tomorrow.

"We've got bc smart about this," Brakes murmured. "The people involved won't sit idle if they catch wind of what we're doing."

Harris nodded, his gaze turning serious. "And you still don't know the name of the man you brought to the cells?"

"I have pressed him. Even the Chief as had a go at him, but nothing," Brakes explained with a frown. "Not a single word."

They continued to discuss for around twenty minutes, when Brakes' phone began to ring, breaking the moment. He frowned and picked it up. On the other line, he was immediately greeted by one of the constables from the holding cells.

"This is Brakes," he said into the receiver, and just at that moment, Vera had started making her way toward the desk, having returned from filling up the car.

"Sir, you need to come down here," the constable said, his tone urgent. "It's about the man you brought in with Ann Marsh last night."

Brakes stiffened. "What about him?"

"He's dead, sir. It looks like a suicide, but… well, you'd better see for yourself." Silence followed and immediately, Brakes shot to his feet. Vera stared at him, wide-eyed, while Harris watched on curiously.

"We're on our way," Brakes replied, and put the phone down. He turned to Harris apologetically. "We shall have to meet tomorrow, Harris; duty calls." motioning for Vera to follow, Brakes left the desk and made his way toward the cells.

The holding cells were cold, sterile, and eerily silent when Brakes and Vera arrived. The constable led them down a narrow corridor, the smell of disinfectant strong in the air. They stopped in front of a cell where the body of Ann Marsh's accomplice lay sprawled on the floor, his face pale and contorted in pain.

The constable pointed to a length of leather tied around the man's neck. "He used his belt, sir. Hung himself from the bars. We found him like this minutes ago."

Brakes crouched down beside the body, his eyes scanning the scene. Something didn't feel right. The man had been calm, too calm, for someone facing life in prison or, worse, death. And now he was dead, conveniently silenced before Brakes could question him further. Vera stood by with her arms crossed.

"You think someone got to him?" She asked. Brakes didn't answer right away.

He stood up, looking over the cell carefully, then back at the constable. "Was anyone else in or out of this area before you found him?" The constable shook his head.

"No, sir. The cells are locked down." The constable explained. "Only authorised personnel can get in."

"What the *hell* is going on?"

The Chief's growl of annoyance could be heard down the hallway, his heavy footsteps echoing as he approached the cell. When he finally stopped in front of the door, Brakes could see the displeasure and annoyance evident in his superior's eyes at being interrupted. Brakes quickly brought the Chief up to speed.

"I want this this kept quiet," the Chief instructed, his gaze moving between Brakes, Vera and the constable. "No one is to talk about this to anyone outside of those in this cell, is that clear?"

"Yes, sir," everyone replied.

Brakes turned to the constable, his voice low. "We need to get a closer look at the body. I want a full post-mortem done—something about this doesn't add up."

The constable nodded. "I'll arrange it."

As they left the holding area, Brakes immediately went to check on Ann Marsh as he passed her cell. She looked up at him with a steely, silent gaze—she was still very much alive, thank goodness. Without so much as a nod, Brakes continued on his way, his mind clouded with thoughts.

The timing of the man's death was too convenient, too neat. If someone had wanted to shut him up, they'd done it flawlessly, leaving no trace of foul play—at least, none that could be seen at first glance.

They headed back to Brakes' desk, where the growing web of intrigue threatened to overwhelm them. First, John Marsh's murder, then Oakes. Then there was Ann's smuggling operation, and now, the suspicious death of her accomplice.

The puzzle that Brakes had begun to piece together was slowly falling into place, but the picture he was forming looked far darker than Brakes had anticipated.

Vera leaned against the desk, her face grim.

"Someone's covering their tracks, and fast," she said, her voice barely above a whisper. Brakes nodded.

"Whoever's behind this is pulling strings at every level," he replied gravely. "The accomplice was their loose end, and they made sure to tie it up before we could get to him."

After a moment of silence, Brakes reached for his phone and rang down to the cells. Immediately, he instructed the officer to place a guard outside of Ann Marsh's cell, day and night. Upon ending the call, Brakes stood up and paced the floor while Vera watched silently.

"We're running out of time," he muttered, loud enough for her to hear. "If we don't act quickly, they'll bury every lead we have, or pack up and leave the country"

"We've still got Harris coming back in tomorrow," Vera reminded him, though it did little to ease Brakes' nerves. "From what I have heard, if anyone can follow the money trail, it's him."

Brakes stopped pacing, his gaze steady on Vera. "Right. And we need to keep digging on our end—the Marsh family isn't done with us yet." Returning to his desk, Brakes sifted through his files, his lips set into a grim line.

Just as Brakes sat back down at his desk, the phone rang again. He answered it without hesitation, expecting more bad news. This time, however, it was a voice he vaguely recognised.

"Inspector Brakes?"

"Yes, who's this?" Brakes asked, his curiosity piqued.

"It's Lieutenant Charles Gray from MI5. I believe we need to talk."

Brakes froze. He knew that name. Charles Gray had been an old school friend, but they had not seen one another in years. And had he said MI5? The secret intelligence service rarely involved itself in local police work, unless something far more dangerous was at play. Brakes exchanged a glance with an intrigued Vera, who had heard the name over the line.

"What's this about, Lieutenant?" Brakes asked slowly. Gray's voice returned, calm but firm.

"I'm calling about your investigation into the Marsh family and the smuggling operation," Gray explained coolly, his words crackling over the line. "You've stumbled onto something much bigger than you realise, Inspector, and if you're not careful, it could cost you a lot more than just your case."

Brakes' heart pounded dangerously against his chest. "Go on," he urged. There was a brief pause on the other end before Gray spoke again.

"You've got eyes on you, Brakes. Powerful eyes. And they don't take kindly to people digging into their affairs." And before Brakes could respond, the line went dead.

He lowered the phone slowly, his pulse beginning to race.

MI5. Eyes on him.

The stakes had just skyrocketed.

CHAPTER TWELVE

"Sir?" Said Vera.

Brakes blinked, broken from his reverie. He turned to stare at Vera, who was leaning over the desk, her eyebrows pinched together in concern.

"Sorry, Vera. What did you say?" Brakes asked. Tapping her finger against the desk, Vera repeated the question Brakes hadn't heard while lost in thought.

"What did he say?" She asked carefully, motioning toward the phone. With a heavy sigh, Brakes rubbed the back of his neck and grimaced.

"That was a Lieutenant Gray from MI5. He says we're in over our heads. Warned us to back off." Brakes explained quietly. Vera's face paled.

"MI5?" She repeated, her voice growing small. "I know I am new to police work, but what the hell are they doing getting involved in a smuggling case?"

Brakes shook his head. "I don't know. But if they're involved, it means we're dealing with more than just local criminals." Drawing a deep breath, Brakes lowered his voice and continued. "We're talking espionage, government secrets—things that people would kill to protect."

Vera gasped, and the reality of the situation hit them both like a freight train. Brakes knew he couldn't ignore Gray's warning, but something inside him bristled at the idea of backing down now. He'd spent too long chasing this case to stop just because some shadowy government agency told him to.

He stood up, pacing the floor once again. "We're in dangerous territory, Vera. We've got to be smart about our next move. If we keep pushing, whoever's behind this won't hesitate to take us out of the picture."

"But we're not backing down, are we?" Vera said, crossing her arms. Her eyes hardened with determination.

"No. We've come too far." Brakes stopped pacing, meeting her gaze. "But we need to be careful—play this like a game of chess. Every move has to count.

Brakes' thoughts drifted back to John Marsh. He had been the first casualty in this game. The man had known something, something that had cost him his life. And now they were no longer just investigating a murder or a smuggling ring—they were unravelling a web of corruption that reached into the highest levels of government, and they had no idea who they could trust.

The next morning, Richard Harris returned to the station, a briefcase in hand and a sharp, focused look in his eyes.

"I have a question, Harris; did you inform your boss you were coming up here?" Brakes asked once they were seated at his desk. Harris nodded.

"Of course. It's protocol," Harris replied, setting his briefcase next to his seat.

"And which MI section do you work for?"

Harris chuckled. "Oh, you know better than to ask those kinds of questions, Brakes."

They set to work after that. Brakes wasted no time in bringing Harris up to speed, sharing the financial documents, transaction records and the details of the smuggling ring they had uncovered. Harris listened intently, his fingers tapping rhythmically on the desk as he processed the information. When Brakes finished, Harris leaned back in his chair, a frown creasing his brow.

"You're right. There's something off about these transactions," he murmured, his eyes trailing over the papers that littered Brakes' desk. "They're too clean, too well-hidden. Whoever's behind this knows how to cover their tracks."

"Can you follow the money?" Brakes asked cautiously.

Harris nodded slowly. "It'll take time, but I can trace the accounts. They've gone through a lot of effort to hide where the funds are coming from and to, but there's always a trail if you know where to look."

Brakes exhaled, a small sense of relief flooding through him. "Good. We need to know who is financing this operation, and if it's connected to something bigger."

Harris packed up the files and shot Brakes a knowing look. "I'll get to work on this right away. But be careful, Brakes; whoever's behind this isn't going to let you get too close without a fight."

Brakes nodded, his jaw tightening. He was more than aware of the risks, especially now with MI5 lurking in the background. He wasn't totally sure he could even trust Harris, but they had to keep going.

Once Harris had left the station, Brakes immediately made his way to the Chief's office and updated him on MI5's call the day before. The Chief listened raptly, his frown deepening the more Brakes revealed.

"Be cautious, Brakes," the Chief warned, his voice low. "Move forward with the investigation, by all means, but keep your eyes and ears open at all times."

"Yes, sir," Brakes agreed, and bid his goodbyes to the Chief. Once he left the office, Brakes made his way back to his desk where Vera was waiting for him, curiosity shrouding her eyes.

"Fetch the car, Vera," Brakes said wearily, tiredness already creeping into his bones. Without a word, Vera nodded and removed herself from the desk to do as she was instructed.

It had been a long day, and Brakes was ready to go home and pour himself a stiff drink.

The car bounced slightly as they turned onto the uneven cobblestone street leading into Norwich's city centre. The sun had started to set, casting long shadows across the cities landscape. He could still hear Gray's warning echoing in his mind: *"You've got eyes on you, Brakes. Powerful eyes. And they don't take kindly to people digging into their affairs."*

He clenched his fists. Vera, sensing his mood, remained silent, but her hands gripped the steering wheel just a little tighter. It was as if the both of them were waiting for the other shoe to drop, for someone to make the next move in this dangerous game.

Brakes stared out the window as Vera manoeuvred the car through Norwich's bustling streets. He had always trusted his instincts, but now, with MI5 involved and the Marsh family secrets entangled in something larger, those instincts were screaming at him to be careful.

As they approached Brakes' home, Vera finally broke the silence. "What's our next step, sir? If MI5's involved, we might be walking into a trap. And if what Ann said is correct..." Vera paused and shook her head. "She said this operation was bigger than all of us, sir."

Brakes exhaled, leaning back in his seat. "We have to keep following the money. Richard Harris is tracing the accounts—he'll give us the lead we need.

Whatever John Marsh and his sister were into, it's global. Bigger than we thought."

Vera parked the car outside Brakes' house, cutting the engine. "And MI5? What if they come after us again?"

Brakes turned to her, his eyes dark. "If MI5 wanted us out of the way, we'd already be gone. They're watching, waiting to see what we'll do next." Rubbing the back of his neck, Brakes leaned back in his seat and sighed. "We just need to move fast. Stay ahead."

He opened the car door and stepped out, taking in a breath of the cool evening air. After a moment, he turned back to the car. "Go home, Vera. Get some rest. Tomorrow, we regroup."

Vera hesitated, looking up at Brakes. "Are you sure, sir? It's getting more dangerous by the day."

Brakes smiled, but it didn't reach his eyes. "I'll be fine. I've handled worse."

She nodded, though the concern in her eyes remained, and drove off. Brakes watched her car disappear into the night before heading inside.

The moment he stepped into his small house, the familiar scent of old wood and motor oil greeted him. The house was quiet, but his mind was anything but.

He tossed his jacket onto a chair, poured himself a glass of whisky, and sat at the kitchen table, staring at the files scattered across it. He couldn't quite believe all that he had stumbled upon regarding the Marsh family since taking on this case. Smuggling, espionage—every new piece of information was like a fresh new puzzle piece, and right now, they were refusing to fit together to form a bigger picture.

Brakes took a long sip of his drink, the liquid burning down his throat, and his thoughts drifted back to John Marsh. The man had been desperate, too deep in something that he clearly could not handle. But what exactly had he uncovered?

His thoughts were interrupted by a sharp knock at the door. Brakes frowned, checking his watch. It was too late for visitors. He stood up, his body tense, and moved cautiously toward the door.

When he opened it, he found a tall, broad-shouldered man dressed in a dark overcoat. The dim streetlight cast shadows over his face, but Brakes recognised him immediately.

Lieutenant Gray.

The MI5 agent's eyes were cold, calculating. He didn't wait for an invitation, stepping inside without a word. Brakes shut the door behind him, watching as Gray scanned the room with the intensity of a predator.

"Cosy," Gray remarked, though there was no humour in his tone. He turned to face Brakes, his expression unreadable. "We need to talk."

Brakes crossed his arms. "I thought you made it clear earlier: Stay out of your way."

Gray's lip curled into a thin smile. "I did. But things have changed."

Brakes felt a chill run down his spine. "What's this about?"

Gray moved toward the kitchen table, glancing over the scattered papers and documents. "You're digging into something far more dangerous than you realize, Brakes," Gray explained coolly, and Brakes narrowed his eyes. "John Marsh was involved with a group that's operating on both sides of the war. They're playing the Allies and the Axis for their own gain."

"And what does MI5 want with them?" Brakes asked and Gray's smile vanished, his expression turning serious.

"They're not just running contraband—They're selling information. Classified intelligence. They've infiltrated our ranks, and now, they're moving in the shadows, pulling strings where they see fit." Gray paused, waiting for a reaction from Brakes. When he didn't get one, he continued. "We've been watching them for years, but we've never gotten this close. John Marsh... Well, he got too close."

Brakes felt his heart beat faster. "So, John was working for them?"

Gray shook his head. "No. He thought he was working for the British government, helping in the war effort. But the people he was dealing with, they're playing a different game. They used him, and when he became a liability, they had him killed."

"And now you're here because you think *I'm* getting too close."

"You are," Gray admitted grimly. "We can't afford to let them disappear again. So, I'm offering you a chance, Brakes: Keep going, follow the trail, but from this point on, you're not just working for the local police. You're working for MI5."

Brakes stared at the agent, weighing his options. The thought of working with MI5 made his skin crawl, but the alternative was worse: Walking away and letting the people responsible for John Marsh's death escape justice.

Gray held out his hand. "Do we have a deal?"

Brakes hesitated for only a moment before clasping Gray's hand.

"We do."

CHAPTER THIRTEEN

The next morning, Vera arrived at Brakes' house, unaware of the storm that had rolled in the night before. Brakes was already dressed, a look of determination set on his face as he drank his tea.

She raised an eyebrow at his demeanour. "You look like you've had a revelation."

Brakes nodded, setting his cup down. "I had a visitor last night. MI5."

Vera's eyes widened, and Brakes quickly filled her in on Gray's visit and the new revelations about John Marsh's true involvement. When he finished, Vera fell into the seat across from him, processing the information.

"So, what now?" She asked, her voice low.

"Now, we follow the money," Brakes replied. "Harris is digging through the accounts. Once we have the names, we'll know who's behind this."

"And MI5? Are we really going to work with them?"

"We don't have a choice. They want us to keep going, but we're in their game now." Brakes exhaled, rubbing his temple. "We have to be careful."

Vera stood, her resolve solidifying. "Then let's do this. Whatever it takes."

Brakes smiled grimly. They were in deeper than ever, but now, they had allies in high places—and enemies in even higher ones.

As they headed out the door, Brakes felt the weight of what lay ahead. The path was dangerous, the stakes higher than he'd ever faced, but he was ready. He had come too far to stop now.

The truth was out there, and he was going to find it—even if it meant risking everything.

Brakes and Vera made their way through the crowded streets of Norwich, the city bustling with wartime activity. The everyday chatter of civilians was drowned out by the rumbling military trucks in the street, and the occasional distant air-raid siren created a backdrop of tension that simply refused to fade.

Vera glanced over at him as she drove. "Where to first?" She asked, gripping the steering wheel tightly. Brakes pulled out the list of addresses he'd jotted down during their tailing of the young man on the motorcycle.

"First, we check these locations—we're going to find out why that lad was making so many stops around town," he explained, carefully reading over the list. "There's something hidden in plain sight, and we're missing it."

They started at the first address, a small, unassuming shop on the outskirts of town. It was a greengrocer's, with crates of vegetables stacked neatly outside the door. The owner, an elderly man with wire glasses, greeted them with a nod as they entered.

"Good morning," Brakes said, flashing his badge. "Just a few questions, if you don't mind."

The old man raised an eyebrow but nodded. "What's this about, officer?"

"There was a young man on a motorcycle making deliveries here recently, wasn't there?" Brakes inquired, gauging the man's expression. "British uniform but riding an American bike."

The old man's face crinkled in thought. "Oh, yes. That lad. He comes around every now and then. Doesn't buy much, just checks in on me, asks how business is. Nice enough fella. Strange uniform, though. I figured he was just one of those boys who got transferred between units."

Brakes frowned. "Did he ever bring anything with him? Or take anything from the shop?"

The old man shook his head. "Nope, never. Just a quick visit, then off he goes."

Brakes exchanged a glance with Vera. A dead end.

"Thank you for your time," Brakes said and turned to leave. As they got back in the car, Vera spoke up.

"So, he wasn't picking up or dropping anything off. What's the point of all these stops then?" She asked curiously. Brakes was silent for a moment, thinking.

"Maybe it's not about the goods. Maybe it's about the people." Brakes said, leaning against the passenger seat. "He's making rounds, checking on certain individuals. Could be that the people he visits are part of something larger—something connected to the smuggling ring."

Vera nodded. "Makes sense. But what are they hiding? And why the strange, unfitting uniform?"

"That's what we need to figure out." Brakes glanced down at the list. "Next stop is a house on the far side of town. Let's see if we get any more clues there."

The second address led them to a quiet residential street, the kind where the houses all looked the same—modest, brick structures with small gardens and white picket fences. The house in question had its curtains drawn, giving it an air of secrecy that made Brakes uneasy.

They knocked on the door, and after a few moments, it creaked open just enough for a middle-aged woman to peek through. Her eyes widened slightly when she saw the two of them standing there.

"Can I help you?" She asked, her voice tight with nerves.

Brakes showed the woman his badge. "We're looking into some deliveries made around town. A young man on a motorcycle stopped here recently. We'd like to ask you a few questions about his visit."

The woman's grip tightened on the door frame. "I... I don't know anything about that. You must have the wrong address."

"Are you sure, ma'am? Several people have confirmed he's made stops here before." Brakes explained, studying her face carefully. "We just want to know what he's delivering or picking up."

The woman's eyes darted to the side for a brief second, and Brakes knew she was hiding something.

"Look, we're not here to cause trouble," Brakes said, softening his tone. "We just need to understand what's going on. If you tell us, we can help protect you."

She hesitated, her hand trembling on the door handle. Finally, she sighed and stepped back, opening the door wider. "Come in."

The house was simple but tidy, with a faint smell of cooking lingering in the air. The woman led them to the small living room, where she motioned for them to sit.

"My name's Mrs. Fletcher," she said quietly. "That young man, he's been coming around for a few weeks now. At first, I thought he was just delivering messages from the military, but…" She trailed off, wringing her hands.

"But what?" Brakes asked gently.

"I overheard him talking to someone outside the house once." She looked down, shame written across her face. "He didn't see me watching, but he was speaking in German."

Brakes' heart skipped a beat. "German?"

Mrs. Fletcher nodded. "I don't understand much of it, but I know enough to recognise the language. He was meeting someone, an older man in a long coat. I didn't see his face, but I knew something wasn't right." She paused, her breath shuddering at the memory. "After that, I stopped answering the door when he came. I don't want any part of whatever they're doing."

Brakes leaned forward, rapt with attention. The young man hadn't been running ordinary errands, as Brakes had feared—he was delivering messages, possibly intelligence, to a network of spies.

"Did you recognise the older man?" Vera asked. "Anything about him stand out?"

Mrs. Fletcher shook her head. "No. He kept his face covered, and I didn't want to get too close. But I think they're using the young man as a courier."

Brakes exchanged a glance with Vera.

"Thank you for telling us," Brakes said, standing. "We'll make sure you're safe, Mrs. Fletcher."

She looked up at him, relief flickering in her fear-stricken eyes. "Please, just make them go away. I don't want any trouble."

Brakes gave her a reassuring nod, and they left the house. As soon as the door closed behind them, Vera turned to him.

"This is getting worse by the minute, sir," she whispered.

Brakes clenched his jaw. "If the Germans have people embedded here in Norwich, MI5 must already know about this. They probably already have their eyes on half the town."

Vera frowned. "Then why haven't they done anything about it?"

"Because they're using us," Brakes said with a shake of his head. "They want to see how deep this goes, and they're hoping we'll flush out the players."

"And we're the bait," she whispered, her face hardening.

"Exactly," Brakes replied grimly. "But now we have leverage; we know the game they're playing. The only question is, how do we stay one step ahead?"

Later that night, Brakes sat in his dimly lit living room, poring over the notes and files in front of him. The young man on the motorcycle was unwittingly—or knowingly—caught in a web of espionage, delivering messages between German spies and their contacts in Britain.

It was clear that John Marsh had somehow gotten too close to this operation, entangled in something he could not handle. It was a deadly game, one that Brakes had inadvertently stumbled into, but it was one he intended to survive.

His thoughts were interrupted by the sound of the phone ringing. He stood, picking up the receiver.

"Inspector Brakes," he answered. There was a pause on the other end of the line, and then a familiar voice spoke.

"Brakes, it's Richard Harris. I've found something." Harris said, his voice tense. "You need to see this—now."

Brakes' stomach tightened. Harris rarely called out of hours unless it was something big, or perhaps dangerous.

"What is it?" He asked, his voice low.

"The money trail. It leads somewhere… unexpected. I'll explain when you get here." Harris' tone was final, and the line went dead.

Brakes hung up the phone, his pulse quickening. If Harris had found something, it meant they were finally on the right track. He had been digging into the financial side of the investigation for a day or two now, and the truth was already within reach. But it also meant that the people they were chasing were getting closer, too.

Brakes phoned Vera for a lift. It was late, but it couldn't be helped. Grabbing his hat and coat, he stepped out into the brisk night air. The quiet streets of Norwich were a stark contrast to the turmoil that swirled within.

When Vera pulled the car up, Brakes slipped into the passenger seat, only reciting an address for them to go to. They drove in silence, the rhythmic hum of the engine echoing through the interior.

As they approached Harris' office, a small light flickered through the smallest of gaps in the curtains. *"He'll get into trouble for that if one of the ARP men see this."* Brakes thought, and felt a knot of unease tightening in his chest.

Vera parked, and they both stepped out into the stillness of the street. The air was cool, but the undercurrent of tension made it feel stifling. Brakes walked up to the door and knocked softly, exchanging a glance with Vera as they waited.

The door creaked open, and Harris stood there, looking even more dishevelled than usual. His tie hung loosely around his neck, his eyes bloodshot, but his expression was one of barely contained excitement.

"Come in," he said, motioning for them to quickly come inside.

The office smelled of stale coffee and old books. Papers were strewn across the desk, along with a few ledgers and a stack of telegrams. Harris hurried over to his desk, fumbling through the mess as Brakes walked straight over to the curtains and closed them tightly while Vera stood by, watching him.

"Alright, what have you found?" Brakes asked, cutting straight to the point.

Harris pulled out a sheet of paper from the bottom of the pile and handed it to Brakes. "It's a bank statement. I've been going through the financials of John Marsh's estate. At first, everything seemed legitimate—inheritances, investments, even a few risky ventures. But then I found *this*."

Brakes studied the statement. It showed large sums of money being moved in and out of accounts with alarming frequency, amounts that didn't line up with Marsh's known assets or lifestyle.

"What's this connected to?" Brakes asked, his brow furrowing.

"That's the thing," Harris replied, sitting down heavily in his chair. "The money isn't going to any of Marsh's businesses or personal investments. It's being funnelled into a series of dummy accounts. Shell companies. I traced one of them back to a shipping firm—guess where?"

Brakes didn't answer. He already knew where this was headed.

"Germany," Harris finished. "Specifically, an account in Berlin that's linked to a known smuggling syndicate operating out of the port. And it's not just any syndicate, Brakes. This one has ties to the Abwehr—German military intelligence."

Brakes felt a chill run down his spine. So, this was it—the smoking gun. John Marsh was moving money for a German spy ring, and that meant he hadn't just been killed by opportunistic thieves; he'd been silenced.

"Marsh was moving money for the Germans?" Vera asked, her eyes wide with disbelief.

Harris nodded. "Looks that way. At first, it seems like he might've been cocrccd—maybe blackmailed. But then I found something else."

He reached into his drawer and pulled out a small, leather-bound journal. It was old and worn, the pages yellowed with time. "This was found in Marsh's desk. It's encrypted—mostly gibberish. But I managed to crack some of the code."

Brakes' palms sweated with eager anticipation as he flipped open the journal. The pages were filled with rows of numbers and cryptic symbols, but Harris had circled certain sections where the patterns broke.

"He was keeping track of the payments. Every time he made a transaction for the Germans, he recorded it here. But there's more." Harris' voice dropped to a whisper. "The journal also mentions a meeting, a crucial one that was supposed to happen just before he was killed."

"What kind of meeting?" Brakes asked desperately, leaning forward.

"A hand-off," Harris said. "Marsh was supposed to deliver something—a package or some information. He doesn't specify, but whatever it was, it was enough to get him killed."

"So, Marsh wasn't just an unwilling pawn. He was actively working with them?" Vera asked, glancing at Brakes.

"Looks that way," Brakes muttered. "But the question is, what was he delivering? And who was supposed to receive it?"

Harris tapped the journal. "There's a location mentioned in the final entry. An old warehouse near the docks. Marsh was supposed to go there the night he was murdered."

Brakes felt a surge of adrenaline. This was the break they needed.

"We're going to that warehouse," Brakes said, standing up abruptly. "If Marsh was supposed to deliver something, it might still be there. And if the Germans are involved, they'll be watching it."

Vera nodded, already moving toward the door. "I'll get the car ready."

Harris looked up at Brakes, concern etched into the lines of his face. "Be careful, Brakes. If you're right about this, you could be walking into a trap."

"I've got no choice, Harris. If Marsh was tied to the Germans, then they're already watching me. Might as well meet them on my terms." Brakes walked toward the door and gave Harris a grim smile. "Can you ring the station and ask them to wake everyone? This time, we are not going in alone."

They left Harris' office quickly, barely speaking as Vera drove them to the address Harris had found. The warehouse was located on the edge of the docks, a hulking structure that had seen better days. It was surrounded by piles of old shipping crates and rusted machinery, the perfect place for something—or someone—to disappear.

Vera parked a few streets away, and they approached the warehouse on foot, keeping to the shadows. The moon hung low in the sky, casting an eerie light over the scene.

"Looks abandoned," Vera whispered as they crouched behind a stack of crates.

"Maybe," Brakes muttered. "But if Marsh was supposed to deliver something here, they wouldn't just leave it unguarded."

As he moved closer to the building, he gestured to Vera to stay put and wait for the uniforms to arrive, his eyes scanning the perimeter. The front doors were locked, but there was a small side entrance that appeared slightly ajar. He crept toward it, listening for any signs of life inside.

Just as he reached the door, Brakes heard a faint click behind him.

"Don't move."

Brakes froze. The voice was low, cold, and unmistakably German. Slowly, he raised his hands, turning to face his captor.

A man stood in the shadows, his pistol trained on Brakes. He was tall, with sharp features and slicked-back hair that screamed military discipline, and his expression was unreadable.

"You've been very persistent, Inspector," the man said, his voice dripping with disdain. "But this is where your investigation ends."

Brakes stared him down, all while trying to figure a way out. "You must be the one Marsh was working for," he said, keeping his voice even. "What were you expecting him to deliver?"

"That's none of your concern anymore." The man said, his lips curling into a thin smile. "You've meddled too much already."

Before Brakes could respond, there was a sudden movement from the shadows. *Vera.*

Moving silently and swiftly, she emerged from behind the crates, her hand clamping down on the man's wrist. With a sharp twist, she disarmed him before he could react, the gun clattering to the ground.

The man snarled and immediately turned to lunge at Vera, but Brakes was quicker. He tackled the man to the ground, pinning him down as Vera grabbed the gun and aimed it at their captive.

"Don't even think about it," she hissed.

Hauling the man to his feet, Brakes made sure to keep a firm grip on his arms. "You're going to tell us everything." He growled, tightening his hold. "Who's behind this, and what were you after?"

The man sneered. "You think you've won, Inspector? There are more of us, and you'll never stop what's coming."

"We'll see about that." Brakes narrowed his eyes, his anger rising as he slapped a pair of cuffs on the man. But deep down, he knew the man wasn't bluffing—this was just the tip of the iceberg. The real threat was still out there, lurking in the shadows and waiting to strike.

As Brakes pushed the man forward, a sound caught Brakes' attention from within the warehouse. Vera's head swivelled toward the noise, her gaze focused on a particular spot.

"There's more of them inside, sir." She said, and Brakes shot her an exasperated look, as though to say, *"No, do you think?"*

"Stay here and cover him and wait for the uniforms." Brakes instructed firmly, waiting for Vera to nod in agreement. "And this time, do as I say, Vera."

Taking care to stay in the shadows, Brakes slowly made his way inside the warehouse with his pistol drawn. The place was massive, meaning that the culprits could be anywhere, but he still searched every corner he came across, each move carefully placed while he looked.

Then, he heard it: Movement, except now it was behind him. Pointing his weapon in front of him, Brakes determinedly moved back over the ground he had already covered and prowled through the dark.

He could hear voices, low and soft, and unmistakably male. They were so low, in fact, that Brakes couldn't make out a word that was being said. Still, he moved, making his way back towards the door he had entered. Clearing a grate, Brakes felt relief wash over him for making it out safely, only for his heart to jump into his throat when someone grabbed him by the wrist and started to wrestle for his pistol.

Another person grabbed him from behind, grunting when Brakes pushed back. He felt a rush of air against his head, and Brakes was dimly aware of his hat being knocked off, now lost to the darkness that surrounded him and his assailants. Then, an arm slipped around his neck, and Brakes started gasping for breath.

Was this it? Would this be the end of him? *"No. Not now,"* he thought. Not when he had come so far. Through sheer stubbornness, Brakes tightened his grip on his pistol while his attacker tried to pry the gun from his grasp.

"Drop it!" The man yelled, clearly annoyed. "Police!"

At the sound of his attacker's voice, Brakes began to relax enough to breathe a little easier despite still being locked against the second officer. He did not let go of his pistol, however—that was the one thing he refused to surrender.

"It's Brakes," he wheezed. "Inspector Brakes. Let me go, you fools."

At the sound of his voice, the two uniformed officers faltered for a moment, clearly surprised. Then, slowly, they let him go and moved to turn on their torches to find Brakes, now desperately trying to catch his breath while simultaneously scanning the ground for his hat. He gave up, however; it was too dark to locate his beloved fedora.

"Ah." One of them muttered, looking down at the ground guiltily. "Sorry, Inspector."

"You have just given our position away." Brakes snarled, glaring at both officers coldly. "Well done."

The second officer, the one that had tried to take Brakes' pistol, shook his head in disagreement.

"Doesn't matter, Inspector. No one is getting out of here." He explained calmly. Brakes' eyebrows rose. "We have the place surrounded."

At his words, a bevy of activity began. The sharp trill of police whistles filled the air, followed quickly by the shouts of various men and persistent footsteps echoing throughout the warehouse. Torch lights shone through the dark, lighting the space like a West End show.

If an air raid were to happen in that moment, then they were all surely in for it, Brakes thought.

Leaving the officers to their job, Brakes stepped back outside and made his way over to Vera, who had thankfully stayed put with their captive. The man glared at Brakes, but he ignored him. With an incline of his head, she followed him back to the car where they shoved the man into the backseat and slammed the door shut behind him.

Thankfully, it didn't take long for the uniformed officers to round up the people inside. From the car, both Brakes and Vera watched as the officers marched out of the warehouse one by one, but the sight that greeted them was shocking.

Boys. Young boys, all trailing after the uniformed officers by the scruff of their necks. Why, they couldn't have been any older than ten, eleven years old? What were they even doing in the warehouse, and so late at night, Brakes wondered.

There were eight of them in total. Once they had all filed out of the warehouse, Brakes called over a free officer before turning to the man on the backseat of the car and opened the door.

"Get out," he growled gesturing for the man to move quickly. He did as he was told, and Brakes handed him over to the uniformed officer.

"Take them all back to the station." Brakes instructed. The officer gave him a stiff nod and marched the man toward the other uniforms immediately. Turning back to Vera, Brakes sighed, already feeling tired from the events.

"Stay with me for now, Vera. I want to take another look around the warehouse, now that it's clear."

Grabbing a couple of torches from the boot of the car, they both headed inside. The first thing Brakes wanted to look for, of course, was his hat. Thankfully, it didn't take long to find it—in fact, it was Vera who had picked it up while traversing through the crates.

"Your hat, sir." She said, perhaps a little sheepishly, and handed Brakes his dusty, crushed fedora.

"I—I can't believe this." Brakes muttered, appalled. "Look at it! Flat as a pancake." Grumbling to himself, Brakes took the hat from Vera shook his head. "One of those big-hoofed, uniformed flatfoots must have trampled on it."

Beside him, Vera hummed in agreement while Brakes reformed and dusted off his hat. He did not see the guilty smile on Vera's lips, however, nor would he find out that it was, in fact, *her* foot that stepped on his hat moments before finding it.

Placing his hat back onto his head, Brakes continued his search throughout the warehouse with Vera by his side. It seemed as if the place was full of empty crates, however, and Brakes cursed under his breath at his luck.

And then he stumbled upon it. A lone American motorcycle, standing proudly in the darkness and gleaming beneath their torchlight.

"Well, well, well," Brakes said, the corners of his mouth ticking upwards into a triumphant smile. "Hopefully two of those little bastards heading back to the station are the lads I have been chasing around the town."

Vera looked at him curiously. "Sir?" She asked, but Brakes ignored her and continued muttering to himself.

"We'll find out soon enough," he said. Finally, he turned to Vera, a renewed jump in his step. "Back to the station, Vera. We have children to question."

CHAPTER FOURTEEN

Brakes sat in the interrogation room, the dim light casting long shadows across the table. The German agent, whom they had wrestled to the ground at the warehouse, sat opposite him, hands cuffed, his cold gaze fixated on the floor. Vera stood by the door, arms crossed, her eyes locked on their prisoner.

They had barely gotten any information out of him in the last two hours. His arrogance was frustrating, and each time they pressed him about the operation, he would sneer, a defiant smirk playing on his lips. They were no closer to understanding the full extent of the network operating within their own town.

"I don't think you're going to get anywhere, he seems totally resolute." Vera whispered to Brakes during a short break. Brakes leaned back in his chair and rubbed his temples in frustration.

"If only I could get him talking, I am sure he has vital information. But he also knows we can't break him in time." Brakes muttered and wearily shook his head. "There's something happening. Something soon. I can feel it, Vera."

Heading back into the integration room, Brakes stared at the man across the table, his thoughts running through the limited leads they had. They had already managed to disrupt one part of the operation, but taking out one or two pawns would not fell the major players.

Brakes slammed his good hand down hard on the table, causing the man to look up, startled. His smirk faltered for just a second, but it wasn't enough for Brakes to get him talking.

"You think you're clever, don't you?" Brakes growled, leaning forward. "You think your friends will come for you? Or maybe you've already set things in motion, and we're just wasting our time. But I promise you this—you won't leave here until you tell me exactly what's going on."

The agent remained silent, his expression hardening. Brakes leaned in even closer, dropping his voice to a dangerous whisper.

"What was Marsh supposed to deliver? You've already lost whatever was in that warehouse where we arrested Ann Marsh, and we have your team of youngsters in a cell. But if you tell me what you're after then maybe, just maybe, you won't rot in a cell for the rest of your life."

The German's face betrayed nothing, but there was a slight shift in his posture, a tightening of his jaw. Brakes caught it instantly. That what something he could build on. He stood up, pacing around the room, letting the silence build.

"You think we don't know about your network, about the smuggling operations? We do. What we don't know is who you're working with on this side. And believe me, we will find out." Brakes warned him, his gaze penetrating as he watched over the agent.

"Did you know that one of your own people was murdered, right here, in one of our cells? They might come for you next."

The agent's eyes followed Brakes as he circled the room, his smirk long gone. There was something in his eyes now—perhaps doubt, maybe even fear. Brakes could work with that.

"You might think you're a martyr for your cause," Brakes said, his voice steady and low. "But in reality, you're just another pawn. Someone higher up will replace you, and no one will care what happens to you."

For the second time, the man shifted in his chair, his confidence wavering.

"You're not protecting anyone important." Brakes continued, his voice growing more forceful. "Just names on a list. They'll forget about you the moment you're caught. But if you help us now, we can make sure you're remembered. That you don't just disappear into the system, or worse—get killed."

The agent's eyes narrowed, but his silence stretched. Vera moved from her position near the door and placed a hand on Brakes' shoulder.

"You can sense it, can't you?" She said softly, addressing the agent. "Your network is crumbling. There are cracks, and the British forces are closing in. This operation you're protecting is falling apart, and you're here. Alone."

There was a flicker of hesitation in the man's gaze. Vera leaned in closer.

"We found Marsh's journal." She said quietly. "We know about the meeting. We know he was supposed to hand over something crucial the night he was killed, and we know that your people panicked when he didn't show up. You're already losing ground, so just tell us what you were after."

The German agent clenched his fists, his knuckles turning white, but still, he didn't speak. Brakes exchanged a quick glance with Vera. It was time to try another angle.

"Fine." Brakes said, throwing his hands in the air. "We'll do it your way."

He gestured for Vera to follow him, leaving two burly uniformed officers to watch over the German agent, and left the room. The door clicked shut behind them as they stepped into the dimly lit hallway. There, Harris was waiting, leaning against the wall, his arms crossed.

"Any luck?" Harris asked, his expression grim.

"Not yet," Brakes muttered, rubbing his eyes. "He's tight-lipped, but he's scared—he knows we're closing in. Something's happening soon, I can feel it in my bones. and we still have no idea what they're planning."

Harris sighed, nodding in agreement. "I've been digging into Marsh's contacts. There's someone who stands out—an Edward Kingsley. He's a businessman, well-respected, but there's something off about his recent transactions. Large amounts of money moving around, all tied to shell companies, just like the ones Marsh was using."

"Kingsley?" Brakes frowned. "I've heard that name before. He's got ties to the shipping industry, hasn't he?"

"That's right. And I've found connections between him and several other key figures who may be involved in the smuggling ring." Harris confirmed. "If he's involved, it could be bigger than just espionage. Kingsley has the influence and resources to move goods across borders without raising too many questions, and not just in Europe, either."

"So, neither of the Marsh family were just middlemen." Vera said, realisation dawning on her. "They were working for Kingsley."

"That's what it looks like." Harris replied. "But we need more than just speculation—we need proof."

"I'll pay him a visit in the morning, but we'll need backup. If he's involved, he won't go down easily." Brakes said firmly. "Right, then—let's see if we can put the fear of God into these lads down in the cells. They must know some of what is going on. At the very least, we will find out their part in it all."

"Understood, sir." Vera said with a determined nod. "Shall we go down to the cells?"

Brakes shook his head. "No. I will be going alone. You two stay here; watch over our friend in there. I should be back shortly." And with that he left, making his way down to the cells where the group of young lads was being kept.

As Brakes entered the cell area, he asked the officer on duty if any of the lads had said anything. "Nothing," was the quick and simple reply. Motioning over to the two biggest, roughest looking uniformed officers, Brakes had them both follow him downstairs. Their purpose? To simply stand behind him without saying a word. Intimidation was the name of the game, here.

"Right, lads; who's gonna be first, then?" Brakes asked, staring into the cell and scanning over the cluster of boys. His eyes narrowed, and a fresh wave of fear rippled across each of their faces while they looked back at him. Then, one by one, each lad stared down at their shoes in a bid to shy away from Brakes' gaze.

All but one, Brakes noticed. Turning to the officers, he pointed towards the lad that was still staring up at him and nodded.

"Grab that one," he instructed them gruffly, jerking his head in the direction of the kid. "Bring him up to interrogation."

Unceremoniously, the officers wrestled the lad out of the cell by the scruff of his neck and practically dragged him towards the interrogation room. Brakes didn't bother to look back at the remaining children and followed the two officers.

Once the young lad had been deposited into the interrogation room, Brakes closed the door firmly behind him and wasted no time on the boy.

"Right, laddie," Brakes snarled, his glare dark. "Name and age?"

The lad muttered something, only to stop immediately, as if contemplating his answer or remembering that he had been told to say something else. After a moment, he spoke up.

"George," he started, a tang of an accent lacing each syllable. "12, sir."

Brakes paused, wondering what the lad had said, exactly. He asked the boy to repeat himself, his voice growing louder, and the boy sat up straight in his seat. After a deep breath, he repeated his name and age, his voice and English much clearer this time.

Brakes would be certain to not forget the lads first attempt, however, and he did not believe for one moment that George was this child's real name.

"You're in some very serious trouble, George." Brakes explained, his voice eerily calm and even. "You're the right age to go to prison, too, and for a very long time. Espionage in this country is taken very seriously, and you and your mates are in this up to your necks."

"Prison?" The boy looked up at Brakes, confusion clear on his face. "No, I will be sent back home. They told me that you would send me home."

Brakes shook his head. "Yes, prison. You'll never see your parents again, or your friends, for that matter." Placing his clenched fists on the table, Brakes bore down on the lad, who leaned back in his seat uncomfortably. "Who told you this? Your mum and dad?"

"No, not my parents." The lad replied, a tremor in his voice. "At the school. They told me you would send me home."

"What school?" Brakes asked.

The boy hesitated for a moment. "Our school. The one we all went to in... in..." He stopped there and fell silent, his eyes growing wide and fearful. It was clear that the lad was too scared to divulge the truth to Brakes. Taking the seat across from the young lad, Brakes clasped his hand together and looked the boy straight in the eyes.

"This can take as long as you want it to, boy. The sooner you tell me everything, the sooner you and your friends will get some hot food and drink. Now, which school?" Brakes pressed, and the boys' eyes flashed with what Brakes suspected to be intrigue and hunger.

A moment of silence settled between them, the only sound in the room an erratic tapping of the boy's foot. Finally, after contemplating over what he could say next, the boy gave Brakes his answer.

"The—the one in…" The boy swallowed and looked nervously around the room. Letting out a shaky breath, his voice returned, this time much smaller, though his accent seemed heavier again. "The one in Germany, sir."

Brakes took a sharp breath and rubbed both hands over his face. *"Just what the hell is going on?"* He thought. There were eight German lads in the cells, some of them barely old enough to spell their own names, let alone understand what the word espionage meant. This case was truly becoming one for the books, it seemed.

He stood up and began pacing the length of the room, trying to make sense of it all. It was a revelation—the German's were training twelve-year-old children to be spies and sending them behind enemy lines. It was unbelievable, and surely it could not be true.

There was one thing Brakes was sure of, though: He needed to talk to the Chief, immediately.

Brakes turned to the officers, who both seemed just as stunned as Brakes was upon hearing the boy's confession.

"Take him back to the cells and be sure to get those kids a hot meal." He instructed them and got up to leave the room. Once outside, he turned to both Harris and Vera, who had patiently been waiting for him to finish up in the interview room.

"Take our German friend back to his cell." Brakes instructed the nearby officer before turning back to Harris and Vera. "You two, follow me." Brakes walked hurriedly through the station, and they quickly made their way to the Chief's office. Finding no time for politeness, Brakes immediately opened the door and popped his head through the doorway.

"Do you have a moment, sir?" He asked, ignoring the Chief's disgruntled look. "You're not going to believe what I have to tell you."

With a heavy sigh, the Chief gestured for them to come in. Brakes closed the door behind Harris.

Brakes took a few moments to compose himself and organise his thoughts. The Chief watched him with a discerning eye, but once Brakes started talking, his superior sat up with keen interest, and the room fell silent.

Shock and horror rippled throughout the room as Brakes explained what he had just found out. Once he had finished, the Chief was already striding around the room, his brow creased in frustration.

"Get MI5 in here right away. This is now out of our jurisdiction—it will have to be handed over to them, immediately." Stated the Chief with a shake of his head. Brakes stiffened, but no one else in the room said a thing.

They were quickly dismissed, and Brakes, Harris and Vera left the Chief's office in silence. Making their way back to Brakes' desk, he slumped down in his chair and sat with his thoughts for a moment.

He ignored Harris and Vera's raised eyebrows and questioning gazes. Instead, he collected himself and pushed back any misgivings about handing the case off to MI5—it was *his case*, for crying out loud!—and reached for the phone to call Gray at MI5.

"Gray speaking." A gravelly voice answered almost immediately. Taking a deep breath, Brakes started speaking into the receiver.

"Gray, it's Brakes. You need to come to the station as soon as possible." He explained. There was silence on the over end of the line for a moment.

"May I ask why?" Gray replied, and even though he couldn't see him, Brakes shook his head.

"Nothing that I can divulge over the phone." He said truthfully. "Be sure to arrive soon. It's urgent." Brakes put the phone down and turned back to Harris and Vera, who were both watching him intently. Sighing mostly to himself, he dismissed them both and got up to make himself a much-needed cup of tea.

It took Gray almost two hours to arrive. By the time he had entered the station, the only people left were the night staff, the Chief and Brakes. The moment Gray walked through the doors, Brakes stood and led him into the Chief's office.

Once Gray had been informed of Brakes' findings, including the money trail they had been following and Kingsley's suspected involvement, all three of them had a long discussion on how best to proceed going forward.

"It would be best if MI5 took over the case from here." The Chief explained to Gray, who nodded in understanding. "However, I insist that you keep

Brakes on. His knowledge will be invaluable, and he can lend outside perspective, of that I am certain.”

“Certainly.” Gray agreed and looked down at his watch; it was close to midnight, but that did not deter him. “I would like to move forward with this as quickly as possible. Brakes, would you be amenable to bringing that lad back for another round of questioning?”

“Indeed.” Brakes said, and they left the Chief’s office and walked down to the cell area. He asked a guard to grab the lad that he had talked to earlier and bring him up again. As they waited, Brakes and Gray discussed their tactics and ultimately decided that Brakes would take care of the questioning while Gray stayed quiet and observed.

A few minutes later, the boy was escorted back into the investigation room, yawning and looking quite weary. Brakes and Gray followed soon after, only to find the lad sprawled out over the table, fast asleep. Gray immediately slammed the door behind him, causing the lad to jump awake.

He looked around the room, wide-eyed as he focused on Brakes and Gray standing in the doorway, their backs ramrod straight as they stared down at the young lad.

“Right, boy.” Brakes began sternly, staring down at the lad. “Tell us your real name, and don’t think about lying to me again.”

The boy looked between them both, contemplating his next answer. Thankfully, the lad seemed to value honesty this time around.

"Carl, sir." He replied quietly, his gaze unwavering. "My real name is Carl Schmidt."

"And how long have you and the others been in Britain?" Brakes enquired. Carl blinked and looked down at his hands, as if trying to calculate the time that had passed on his fingers. When Carl looked up again, he was frowning.

"Um, almost a year, I think?" He thought about his answer, his gaze rising to the ceiling before he looked back at Brakes and Gray. "Yes. Almost a year."

Carl yawned again and looked ready to fall back onto the table. Brakes turned to Gray and gave him a curt nod, and the MI5 agent immediately left the room. He returned shortly after, a glass of Ribena in his hand. Placing it on the table in front of the boy, Carl looked up at Gray almost hopefully.

Gray nodded his permission and pointed to the drink. It was gone in seconds but seemed to bring some life back to Carl.

"What were your instructions when you came here?" Brakes asked calmly, and the boy only took a moment to answer.

"We was told to cause as much trouble as we could." He explained, his voice a little louder now. "So, we started by stealing peoples shopping and bags, sir."

"Right, so you admit that it was you stealing bags." Brakes summarised, nodding as he took some notes down. "And was it you on the motorcycle I chased a few weeks ago?"

"Yes, sir," The lad confirmed. Brakes pressed on.

"What else did you do, Carl?"

"I would ride around and visit people. I don't know why, they just told me to do it."

Brakes stopped scribbling down notes and looked up at the child. "They?" He asked. "Who are 'they'?"

"The man you caught at the warehouse, sir." Carl said without hesitation. "That's it. That's all we did."

With a final nod, Brakes closed his notebook and slipped it back into his pocket. "That will be all, lad." He said and nodded toward the officer that was standing by. "Take the boy back to his cell. He will need his rest, I am sure." And with that, the officer marched towards Carl and took him by the arm.

Once they had left the interrogation room and the door had closed behind them, Gray turned to Brakes and congratulated him on a job well done.

It felt almost freeing, to have solved the mystery of the bag snatching and the ill-fitting uniformed lad he had caught almost a week prior. And the fact that they were one in the same and part of a major German espionage game only seemed to make the reveal that much sweeter.

"We should regroup in the morning." Gray declared just as Brakes stifled a yawn. "Get some rest, Brakes, and once again. Well done."

Brakes could only nod in agreement, the events of the day finally wearing down on him. He would focus on the next part of this operation in the morning, and he already knew who the next target on his radar would be.

Edward Kingsley was up to something, and Brakes would not give up until he found out what.

CHAPTER FIFTEEN

The following morning, Brakes found himself standing outside Edward Kingsley's sprawling estate on the outskirts of Norwich. The property was impressive, a testament to the wealth Kingsley had amassed over the years. Yet, the manicured gardens and stately facade belied the dark dealings that Brakes suspected were taking place behind closed doors.

Vera and Gray waited in the car nearby, keeping watch. Brakes straightened his coat and walked up the steps with Harris following close behind, clutching his leather briefcase to his chest. Brakes knocked on the large oak door. It swung open after a few moments, revealing a butler who looked between Brakes and Harris with a cool, detached expression.

"Inspector Brakes." Brakes announced, showing his badge. "I'm here to see Mr. Kingsley. It's urgent police business."

The butler raised an eyebrow but said nothing as he led Brakes and Harris through the opulent halls of the mansion. The air was heavy with the scent of polished wood and expensive cigars, and the quiet hum of classical music echoed from somewhere deeper within the house.

Kingsley was waiting for them in a lavish sitting room, seated in a leather armchair beside a roaring fire. He was a tall, distinguished man with silver hair and sharp, calculating eyes. Even from afar,

Brakes could see that Kingsley's presence was both commanding and formidable all at once.

"Inspector Brakes, and associate." The butler stated as they entered the room. Kingsley rose from his seat to greet them.

"To what do I owe this unexpected visit?" He asked with a firm shake of their hands.

Brakes cut to the chase. "I'm investigating the death of John Marsh," he said, stepping forward. "And I believe you might be able to help me understand the nature of his business dealings before he died."

Kingsley's expression remained neutral as he gestured for Brakes and Harris to sit. "I knew Marsh," he said smoothly, "but I don't see how his death concerns me; he was a businessman, and our dealings were strictly professional."

Brakes sat, his gaze never leaving Kingsley's face. "Marsh was involved in more than just business, Mr. Kingsley. We have reason to believe he was working with foreign agents—smuggling information, goods, maybe even something more dangerous. And we think he was working for someone of higher standing."

"You're making quite serious accusations, Inspector. Do you have any proof?" Kingsley's eyes narrowed, but he maintained his calm demeanour.

"Not yet," Brakes admitted, "but we will. Marsh's journal points to a network—one that involves powerful figures like yourself. We know about the money transfers and the shell companies." Brakes turned to Harris for the paperwork and started fanning the paper in Kingsley's direction. "You're not as untouchable as you think."

Kingsley's mask slipped just a fraction, and Brakes caught a glint of something dark and dangerous flashing in his eyes.

"You're playing a dangerous game, Inspector," Kingsley said, his voice now laced with malice. "You should be careful. Not everything is as it seems in times of war."

"Neither is the law, Mr. Kingsley, and I intend to see justice done." Brakes stood, meeting Kingsley's gaze with cold determination.

As Brakes turned to leave, he could feel Kingsley's eyes boring into his back, but he didn't look back. He had seen enough. Kingsley was certainly involved—Brakes could feel it in his gut. And whatever he was planning, it was about to come to a head.

Brakes stepped out of Kingsley's mansion with Harris following close behind, and a chill ran down his spine.

"Well, that was short and sweet," said Harris, but Brakes paid little attention to him. He had stirred the pot, but Kingsley wasn't the kind of man to get rattled easily. If anything, Brakes knew the businessman would now be preparing to retaliate.

He walked briskly down the long driveway, his thoughts swirling. Involving Kingsley in the investigation changed the entire scope of what they were dealing with. This was no longer just about Marsh or a simple smuggling operation—this was about power and influence that spanned further than local espionage. It was about an underground war being waged within Britain's borders.

Vera and Gray were still waiting in the car, both alert as Brakes and Harris approached. Vera's eyes scanned Brakes' face, searching for a clue on what had transpired.

"That bad, huh?" She asked. Brakes gave a curt nod as he opened the car door and slid into the back seat.

"Kingsley's dirty, no doubt about it. He's hiding something. I've never seen someone so calm in the face of such direct accusations." Brakes exhaled and rubbed the back of his neck. "He knows we're on to him, but he doesn't care. That means one of two things: either he thinks he's untouchable, or he's already put something in motion that's too far along for us to stop."

"Did he give you anything?" Gray asked, turning to face Brakes from the front passenger seat.

"Not directly. He was too slick for that, but there's something in the way he responded—like he's holding all the cards. Whatever Marsh was involved in, Kingsley was at the top. Now we just need the proof."

Vera glanced over her shoulder as she started the car. "So, what's the plan, sir? We can't just sit back and wait for Kingsley to make his move."

Brakes stared out the window, the Norfolk countryside speeding past. He thought for a moment, then turned back to the others.

"We'll keep pressure on him, but from the shadows. Kingsley has resources and connections we haven't even begun to uncover." He paused, thinking over his next words before continuing. "But there's one thing we do know for certain—Marsh was killed because of something he was supposed to deliver. Kingsley's people must be desperate to get their hands on it."

"Any idea what that might be?" Gray asked, frowning.

"No, and you know, for an MI5 agent, you really ask a lot of questions. Aren't you supposed to know everything about everyone?" Brakes said, annoyed.

Harris, noticing Brakes' chagrin, quickly chipped in. "But it's enough for them to kill two of their own, to keep it falling into the wrong hands."

"Then maybe Marsh and Oakes didn't fail in their mission," Vera mused aloud. "Maybe they hid whatever it was before they were killed."

Brakes nodded thoughtfully. "It's possible. And if that's the case, we need to find it before Kingsley does. It could be our only leverage."

"But where do we start, sir? According to the files, Marsh had contacts all over the place. He could have hidden it anywhere," Vera said with an arch of her eyebrow. "Then there's Oakes. Between the two of them, there must be hundreds of people and places, they were very streetwise, it seems like an impossible task, sir."

"We start with his sister, Ann," Brakes said firmly. "If we can break her, we might just get a lead as to what we are looking for and where to look."

Ann Marsh had always been a slippery person, right from the start, but Brakes had also sensed something more lurking behind her grief-stricken facade. He had been right, of course, so it made sense that Ann might be hiding more than she cared for Brakes to know.

"We'll have her brought up for more questioning," Brakes said. "If Marsh left anything behind—any clues or instructions—Ann will know about it."

Once they were back at the station, Brakes asked for Ann Marsh to be brought up to the interrogation room. When she passed his desk, Brakes could see that her face was pale and drawn. In the short time since her brother's death and her days spent in the cells, it seemed that Ann had aged years.

A few minutes later, Brakes made his way toward the interview room. He was followed by Gray, while Vera and Harris were instructed to wait at his desk until they both returned.

"Inspector," Ann greeted him. "More questions, is it?"

Brakes nodded, his eyes scanning over her for any signs of weakness. Unsurprisingly, Ann gave little away and instead turned her attention to Gray, who was leaning against the wall and watching her closely.

"And who is this fine-looking gentleman?" She asked curiously, her gaze sweeping over the length of Gray's body. "I don't believe I have had the pleasure."

Gray ignored Ann's clear appraisal of him, and Brakes slammed his good hand down onto the table to bring her attention back to him.

"We've learned more about your brother's and your dealings," Brakes snarled, and Ann flinched. Her fingers tightened around the edge of the table.

"I... I don't know what you mean. John was—he was an idiot." The facade fell quickly, and Ann's gaze hardened. Of course, Brakes could not detect a hint of remorse in her words. Leaning closer, Brakes lowered his voice so that only Ann could hear him.

"Ann, you and your brother were working with a powerful man named Kingsley. Surely, you were aware of this. Both of you were in deep—smuggling, espionage, possibly even treason." Brakes listed off each conviction, watching as Ann's eyes slowly grew wider. "But it wasn't just for money; there was something specific he was supposed to deliver, and you people killed him because he had a change of heart."

"Quite possibly, Inspector," Ann whispered, and her lips began to tremble as she shook her head. "But then, he... he was a traitor."

"To his country or your cause?" Brakes asked, his tone growing curt. "What did he have that was so important that he had to die?" Brakes' gaze turned cold, and his next words were bitter. "And that's something you're going to pay for, hopefully with your life."

Ann stared at him for a long moment, her face ashen. Then, with a trembling sigh, "Okay. Okay," she murmured, her voice soft. "John had a notebook, but it's just full of gibberish. I couldn't make any sense of it."

"Where is it?" Asked Brakes, his breath catching in his throat. Ann shifted uncomfortably in her seat.

"It's hidden," Ann replied, glancing down at the table. "In a secret compartment in the desk in his study."

Practically jumping from his seat, Brakes marched toward the door and yelled for Vera to bring the car around. Without sparing Ann a second glance, Brakes exited the interrogation room with Gray in tow, and the three of them made their way to the Marsh estate.

The moment they arrived at the estate, Brakes barely acknowledged the elderly woman that had been taking care of the house as he marched through the door and led Gray to the study. Following Ann's instructions, Brakes quickly found the desk's hidden compartment and retrieved the notebook, its leather-bound cover cracked and weathered with age.

Brakes opened it, flipping through the pages and scanning its contents. At first, it seemed like nothing more than Marsh's jumble of thoughts and musings, but then he found it—symbols, numbers, and strange, coded messages written in the margins, different from the ones in the journal Harris had obtained.

"These are coordinates," Gray said, leaning over his shoulder. "Look here, he's written them multiple times."

Brakes nodded, his mind a whirlwind of thoughts. "This is what Kingsley's after. It's not a physical object. It's information. Something valuable enough to get Marsh and Oakes killed."

He closed the notebook. If Kingsley got his hands on it, Brakes already knew that the consequences would be catastrophic. He turned to look at Gray.

"This will need a closer look," Gray said, carefully taking the notebook from Brakes' hands. Brakes could only nod, his mouth suddenly feeling quite dry at what they had just uncovered.

"I agree," he acquiesced, and started making his way to the study door. "And quickly; we're going to make sure that Kingsley gets his just desserts."

Once they returned to the car, Gray immediately began studying the book while Vera struck up the car.

"Once we have returned to the station, I'll take some pictures of the pages and get them over to our guy's," Gray calmly explained, his fingers carefully tracing over Marsh's notes. "We have some of the best cryptologists there. If they can't break it, then I'll have to send it over to Bletchley."

"About time you started to contribute to this case." Brakes muttered under his breath.

Later that evening, as Brakes sat at his desk studying the coordinates and symbols in the notebook, a feeling of unease settled over him. One thing was clear—Kingsley was a far more dangerous adversary than they had imagined, and the operation he was orchestrating was nearing its endgame.

As the night wore on, Vera and Harris worked beside him, combing through the notebook for any additional clues. Brakes could feel a growing sense of urgency in the air that pressed down on them like a storm cloud waiting to break.

"We need to move fast," Brakes muttered, staring at the cryptic symbols in the notebook. "If Kingsley gets to this first..."

"How can he when we have the book?" Vera asked, her eyebrows raising into her hairline. "Without this he has nothing, right? Let's hope that Gray's people come up with something, and fast."

Brakes glanced at the clock. It was well past midnight, but none of them were ready to stop. Every second counted, and they were on the verge of uncovering something huge—something that could not only bring down Kingsley but possibly disrupt a vast underground network of espionage that could stretch across the country.

Brakes nodded. "I'll contact Gray in the morning; see if they have anything." Sighing, he turned a page in the notebook, ignoring the sharp sting behind his eyes. "But for now, let's focus on trying to decode this ourselves. Whatever it is, it's going to lead us straight to Kingsley's operation; I know it."

CHAPTER SIXTEEN

The morning fog hung low over the city, shrouding everything in a pale mist that seemed to swallow sound and light alike. Brakes stood at his kitchen window, staring blankly at the fields. Having only had a couple of hours sleep, his mind was a little hazy. His tea sat untouched on the table behind him. The events of the previous night weighed heavily on his mind. The notebook that Ann had handed over wasn't just a small piece of the puzzle—it was the key.

But the key to what?

The coded messages, the strange coordinates, the intricate symbols scrawled across the margins—John Marsh had been holding something back, something dangerous enough to cost him his life. And now it was in Brakes' hands, along with the responsibility to figure it out before Kingsley or his men could.

He glanced at the clock. Vera would be arriving soon, and they needed to hit the ground running. Brakes needed resources, manpower, and support beyond the small circle he currently operated within.

He had to contact Gray down in London, but the thought gnawed at him. Brakes had always prided himself on handling things quietly, efficiently, but this was different. Kingsley's operation had tentacles far beyond Norwich, reaching into the highest echelons of influence.

A knock on the door startled him from his thoughts. It was too early for Vera to be there, but Brakes wasn't expecting anyone else. He crossed the room and opened the door cautiously, his hand hovering near his service revolver.

It wasn't Vera.

Standing in the doorway stood Gray, dressed in a neatly pressed suit, his eyes cold and unreadable behind a pair of round spectacles. A briefcase hung from his hand, and a slight smile played on his lips, though it didn't reach his eyes.

"Morning, Brakes," Gray said in greeting. He stepped over the threshold.

"I wasn't expecting company this early," Brakes said, closing the door behind him. He motioned for his visitor to take a seat at the table. Gray sighed, opening his briefcase and pulling out a thin file. He slid it across the table toward Brakes.

"Here is what we have found out so far from the notebook. John Marsh wasn't just some small-time smuggler, as suspected. He was part of a larger network, a group that's been working quietly for years to undermine British intelligence operations." Gray explained, pausing only to gauge Brakes' reaction. "We believe he was handling sensitive information that, if exposed, could compromise ongoing efforts to root out German spies operating on our soil. You will find the coordinates marked on a map from his notebook."

Gray then proceeded to pull out a map from his briefcase and spread it across the table, tapping the markings his team had made. Brakes stiffened; his suspicions were now fully confirmed. "So, Kingsley isn't just an opportunist."

"No," Gray said, his voice low. "Kingsley is a traitor. He's been facilitating the passage of intelligence to foreign powers, and we believe he's preparing to make a major move." He stopped, staring at Brakes for a long moment. He offered no reaction, instead choosing to open the file and scan its contents.

It was thin but damning. Photographs, intercepted messages, and a few blurry surveillance images of Kingsley meeting with individuals Brakes didn't recognise. This wasn't just about local smuggling. It was a web of espionage with Kingsley at the centre.

"We've been watching Kingsley for some time, but his operation has been remarkably difficult to penetrate," Gray revealed. "He uses intermediaries like Marsh to keep himself insulated. Marsh's death was a miscalculation on Kingsley's part. It drew attention we might not have otherwise had."

"Why hold all this back, Gray?" Brakes asked, now eyeing him suspiciously. The MI5 agent simply shrugged in response.

"It was up to my superiors to decide what and when we share information. You know how it is, Brakes." Replied Gray.

"Well, you could have told me earlier," Brakes muttered, flipping through the pages. Gray nodded.

"Look, I'm all in now. Our people are working on the pages," Gray said evenly, though it did little to dissuade Brakes' annoyance. "So, from this moment forward, we will do whatever you need to bring Kingsley down. But remember, Brakes: This needs to be handled quietly."

Brakes closed the file and set it down, now focusing on the map. Gray continued.

"The information in that notebook—it's the key to locating Kingsley's central operation. Once we figure it out, we can dismantle the entire network."

Brakes rubbed the back of his neck. "And if we fail?"

Gray's expression darkened. "If we fail, Kingsley will pass on whatever information he's gathered to our enemies, and it could very well turn the tide of the war in their favour. We cannot afford that."

The weight of the situation pressed heavily on Brakes. He had suspected all along that this was bigger than Marsh's murder, but now it felt as if the entire war effort was resting on his shoulders.

There was another knock at the door, and Brakes' heart leapt in his chest. He crossed the room quickly, opening the door to find Vera standing on the step, her brow furrowed in confusion.

"Am I interrupting?" She asked, glancing past Brakes to where Gray sat at the table.

"Not at all," Brakes said, stepping aside. "Come in. Gray and I were looking over some of the paperwork on Kingsley."

Vera looked down at the map spread across the table as Brakes leaned in, tracing his finger over the coordinates route.

"That's where Marsh was headed." He murmured, tapping the map thoughtfully. "He must have hidden whatever he was carrying there."

Vera glanced at the clock. "Then we need to move now."

Brakes agreed, grabbing his coat and his revolver. They had no time to waste. Whatever Marsh had hidden in that warehouse, it was their only chance to stop Kingsley. Gray stood up, clutching his briefcase as he headed for the door.

"I will head back to London to see how the team are doing with the rest of the notebook." Gray said. Brakes nodded and locked eyes with Vera.

"Let's get to work."

Brakes and Vera headed straight to the location that had been marked on the map. It was an unassuming warehouse on the outskirts of Norwich, long abandoned and far enough from the city centre that no one would take notice of activity there.

The drive there was tense, the car cutting through the early morning mist like a knife through butter. The narrow streets of Norwich gave way to more open industrial roads, with each turn opening his mind to what could be waiting for them.

Brakes kept replaying Gray's words over in his head—*this needs to be handled quietly*—but the quiet would only last until they reached the warehouse. Kingsley's men would surely be on alert.

"But why hide something in such an obvious place?" Vera asked, tapping the steering wheel with a frown.

"Because no one would think to look," Brakes replied. "It's too obvious. But that means Kingsley will send his men there soon, if he hasn't already."

Vera kept her eyes on the road, her hands tight on the wheel. "What's the plan when we get there?" she asked, her voice low but firm.

"We assess the situation first," Brakes replied, his gaze never leaving the road ahead. "If Kingsley's men are there, we'll need to be smart about how we approach—no going in guns blazing."

Vera glanced at him, a hint of a smile tugging at her lips. "I don't think I've ever seen you go in guns blazing, sir."

Brakes smirked. "I prefer to save the bullets for when they're really needed."

The warehouse loomed in the distance, a hulking, dilapidated structure surrounded by overgrown brush and rusted fences. It had clearly been abandoned for years, its windows broken and its walls tagged with graffiti. But beneath that layer of neglect, there was a quiet menace—a sense that the building had not been truly forgotten.

Brakes motioned for Vera to slow down as they approached. They pulled off the main road, parking the car behind a cluster of trees just far enough from the warehouse to remain unnoticed but close enough for a quick getaway if needed.

They both stepped out of the car, and Brakes immediately scanned the perimeter. The area appeared deserted, but that meant little in this line of work. If Kingsley had men stationed here, they would be out of sight, likely watching from the shadows.

"Let's take a look around," Brakes whispered, nodding toward the side of the building. They crept forward, sticking close to the tree line, their footsteps muffled by the thick grass.

As they reached the edge of the warehouse, Vera stopped, holding up her hand. Brakes followed her gaze, spotting a figure near the back entrance. The man was tall, dressed in a long coat, with his back turned to them. He was smoking a cigarette, and every so often he glanced around, as if waiting for something—or someone.

"One of Kingsley's men?" Vera whispered.

"Most likely," Brakes replied, crouching lower behind a stack of old crates. "We'll need to get closer, but we can't risk alerting him."

They waited a moment longer, observing the man's movements. He seemed casual enough, but Brakes knew better than to underestimate him. Kingsley wouldn't send just anyone to guard a location as important as this—the man would be armed and ready to act at the slightest provocation.

Vera tugged on Brakes' sleeve. "There's a side window. We could slip in while he's distracted."

Brakes nodded. "Let's move."

They circled around the building, keeping low to avoid detection. The window Vera had spotted was cracked open, and with a gentle push, Brakes eased it open further. He hoisted himself up and into the warehouse, landing quietly on the dusty concrete floor. Vera followed close behind.

Inside, the air was thick with the smell of oil and damp wood. The large, open space was filled with rusted machinery, old crates, and debris scattered across the floor. Sunlight filtered through the broken windows, casting long shadows that danced across the walls.

Brakes motioned for Vera to stay close as they navigated their way through the cluttered space. In the far corner of the room, something caught his eye—a set of crates, newer than the others, stacked neatly and covered with a tarpaulin.

"That's it," Brakes whispered, his heart thrumming against his chest.

They moved toward the crates, and as they neared, Brakes felt the hairs on the back of his neck stand up. Something wasn't right. He stopped in his tracks, his hand instinctively going to his revolver.

Just as he was about to warn Vera, a voice echoed through the warehouse.

"Looking for something, Inspector?"

Brakes froze, turning slowly toward the source of the voice. From the shadows emerged two men, both armed, their pistols trained on him and Vera.

And standing between them, with a self-satisfied grin on his face, was none other than Kingsley. Brakes cursed under his breath—he had walked right into a trap.

"Well, well," Kingsley said, each word dripping with mockery. "I have to say, I wasn't expecting you to show up so soon, Brakes. But I'm impressed. You've certainly caused me more trouble than I anticipated."

Brakes didn't flinch, his gaze locked on Kingsley. "Cut the theatrics, Kingsley. You're done," he hissed, his hand fixed on his revolver. Kingsley chuckled darkly, shaking his head.

"Ah, you still think you've got the upper hand, don't you? How quaint. But no, Inspector, I'm afraid it is you who is finished." All humour left Kingsley's voice, and his gaze hardened. "You've been sniffing around in places you don't belong. Now, you've found your way to my doorstep, but you won't be leaving."

Brakes tried to stay calm while he assessed the situation. Two armed men with Kingsley in the middle. There was no easy way out of this. But he had to stall, buy time to think of a way to turn the tables.

"You're making a mistake, Kingsley," Brakes said, his voice firm and steady. "You think you can keep playing both sides, but MI5 is onto you. They know everything. Your time is up."

Kingsley's smile faltered, but then he regained his composure. "MI5?" he scoffed. "They're as clueless as the rest of them. By the time they realise what's happening, I'll be long gone with everything I need."

"And what exactly do you need?" Brakes asked, his eyes narrowed. "What's so important that you'd kill twice to get it?"

"Marsh was a fool. He didn't understand what he had," Kingsley said, and his eyes gleamed with a dangerous light. "But I do. He stumbled onto something that could shift the balance of power, and now it's mine."

Brakes' grip on his revolver tightened. "And where is it?"

Kingsley took a step forward, his grin widening. "Oh, you'll see soon enough, Inspector. But I'm afraid you won't live to tell anyone about it."

Before Brakes could react, Kingsley's men raised their pistols, ready to fire.

The back door slammed open, and in burst a squad of MI5 agents, led by none other than Agent Gray.

"Drop your weapons!" Gray shouted, his gun raised, flanked by several agents with rifles pointed directly at Kingsley and his men.

He hesitated, glancing between Brakes and the approaching agents, and realised that he had been outmanoeuvred.

Brakes seized the moment, drawing his revolver and stepping forward. "It's over, Kingsley. You're under arrest."

Kingsley's men exchanged nervous glances before slowly lowering their weapons. Kingsley, however, clenched his fists, his face twisted with rage. He turned toward Brakes.

"This isn't over, Brakes. You've only delayed the inevitable," Kingsley spat venomously. Brakes looked unfazed.

"We'll see about that."

As Gray and his team moved in to secure Kingsley and his men, Brakes and Vera exchanged a look of relief. The immediate danger had passed, but the mystery was far from over. Whatever Marsh had discovered, whatever secrets Kingsley had been trying to unearth—it was still out there, hidden somewhere in the wreckage of this operation.

Brakes holstered his revolver and took a step towards to Gray, who gave him a respectful nod.

"Good work, Brakes," said Gray approvingly. "I decided it was better to give you some back up."

Brakes exhaled, his muscles finally relaxing. "Thanks, I was starting to get a little fed up with people pointing guns at me," he said with a bite of sarcasm to his voice. "But there's still more to this than we've uncovered. You know that, right, Gray?"

Gray glanced over at the crates in the corner. "We'll go through everything here. Whatever Marsh was protecting, we'll find it."

Brakes nodded, but a part of him couldn't shake the feeling that this wasn't the end. Kingsley's operation may have been dismantled, but the danger Marsh had hinted at—the coded messages, the coordinates—was still lurking in the shadows, waiting to be revealed.

CHAPTER SEVENTEEN

Brakes sat in one of the interrogation rooms with the door open, the dim light from the lamp casting shadows on the walls as the evening wore on. The events of the day played over in his mind, each detail a puzzle piece, some fitting perfectly together while others remained elusive. Kingsley was now in custody, but his words haunted Brakes.

"This isn't over, Brakes. You've only delayed the inevitable."

Kingsley's operation had been intricate, far-reaching and deadly. But the bigger question that gnawed at him was what Marsh had uncovered what Kingsley so desperately wanted, and that something was still out there.

A knock at the door broke his thoughts. Vera stepped in, carrying two cups of tea. She set one down in front of Brakes before taking a seat across from him.

"You look like you've seen a ghost," she said, studying his face.

Brakes took the tea, though he wasn't in the mood to drink it. He stared down at the dark liquid swirling in the cup. "I can't shake this feeling, Vera. We've got Kingsley, but I don't think we've stopped anything. I believe he was working for someone—or something—much bigger."

Vera nodded in understanding, though she had little to offer outside of that. A moment of silence passed between them. Brakes rubbed his eyes, exhaustion weighing on him. He hadn't really slept in over 24 hours, and the adrenaline that had kept him going was now beginning to wear off. But sleep would have to wait.

"What did the MI5 agents find at the warehouse?" Vera asked, finally breaking the silence.

"They're still going through it. Mostly stolen goods—black-market items—but there were a few documents they're analysing." Brakes explained, his tea left untouched. "Gray said there was some kind of cipher in one of the ledgers, something they haven't been able to crack yet."

"A cipher?" Vera's curiosity piqued. "Do you think that's what Marsh was involved in?"

Brakes considered it. "Maybe. Marsh was clever—too clever to leave something like that unprotected. If he stumbled onto something, he would have hidden it well. But Kingsley didn't kill him for just a few stolen goods. Marsh knew something. Something that could have changed the game."

The door opened again, this time revealing Agent Gray. He looked more dishevelled than usual, his tie loose and his expression tense. He held a folder in his hand.

"Brakes," Gray greeted, his voice carrying a weight of urgency. "We need to talk."

Brakes gestured to the chair next to Vera. "What's going on?"

Gray sat, placing the folder on the table. "We've made some progress on the documents we found in the warehouse. It's as we suspected; Marsh had been tracking Kingsley for months, but it goes deeper. The cipher we found in the ledger—it's not just numbers. It's coordinates."

"More coordinates?" Vera asked, leaning forward.

Gray nodded. "Yes, and we've traced them to a remote location outside of town. An old military installation, long abandoned. But here's where it gets interesting." Gray took a moment to look through the folder and produced some papers. Throwing them down onto the table, he tapped one for Brakes and Vera to look at. "The installation was once used for storing classified materials during the early days of the first world war—experimental weapons, intelligence documents, things that never made it to the public."

"And you think that's what Kingsley was after? Something hidden at that site?" Brakes asked, his breath catching in his throat.

Gray's eyes darkened. "Not just Kingsley. Whoever he was working for was after it, too. Kingsley was just another puppet; he was supposed to retrieve whatever was there and hand it off. We think Marsh got wind of it and was trying to stop it."

"So, what's at the site? What are we dealing with?" Brakes asked, sitting up straight in his chair. Gray hesitated for a moment before answering.

"We're not entirely sure. But from what we've gathered, there were rumours—documents detailing plans for a weapon, something that never made it past the drawing board. A prototype, maybe."

Vera exchanged a glance with Brakes. "A weapon? That's what this is all about?"

Gray nodded. "If the rumours are true, it could be something that would shift the balance of power. And if it falls into the wrong hands…"

Brakes felt a knot forming in his stomach.

"What's our next move?" Brakes asked, his voice steady but laced with tension. Gray opened the folder again and spread out a map on the desk, pointing to a location circled in red.

"This is where the coordinates lead," he explained, his voice a low murmur while Brakes studied the map. "We're going to send a team to the site at first light. We need to secure whatever is there before anyone else can get their hands on it."

There was a beat of silence as Brakes memorised the map, his mind racing.

"What about Kingsley? Has he said anything?" asked Gray. Brakes shook his head.

"He's not talking. We've got him locked up, but he knows we don't have all the answers. He's waiting for us to slip up." Brakes explained. He clenched his fists, feeling the familiar frustration of being one step behind. "We need to move fast. If Kingsley was just a pawn, that means there's someone else out there who knows about this. They won't stop."

Gray stood, gathering the papers and folding the map back into the folder. "Agreed. I'll handle the team and keep you updated. But be ready, Brakes. Once we get to the site, things could escalate quickly."

Brakes nodded, watching as Gray exited the interrogation room. The door clicked shut, and the room fell silent again.

Vera leaned back in her chair, exhaling slowly. "A secret military installation, experimental weapons… it all feels like something out of a spy novel."

"Except it's real," Brakes sighed, rubbing his temples. "And if we don't stop this, it could be catastrophic."

They sat in silence for a few moments longer, the gravity of what lay ahead settling over them. Finally, Brakes spoke, his voice low.

"We'll need to be ready. Whoever is behind this, they won't let us stop them without a fight."

Vera nodded, her expression resolute. "Whatever it takes, sir."

As they prepared to leave the station, Brakes thought back to the map Gray had shown them, the red circle marking the coordinates now burnt into his memory. The abandoned installation held secrets—

secrets that had cost two lives and now threatened to plunge them into something even darker.

"We're not gonna miss this," Brakes said, grabbing his coat from the back of the chair. "We're going to that installation tonight, take a look around before Gray's team even sets foot there in the morning."

"You think that's wise? Shouldn't we wait for MI5?" Vera asked, her eyes widening. "They're better equipped to handle something like this."

Brakes shook his head. "By the time Gray's team gets there, whoever's behind this could have already made their move. We need to see what's really there before anyone else does."

Vera hesitated, but then nodded, standing up and slipping on her own coat. "Alright, sir. If we're going, we need to be prepared."

They gathered what little gear they had, including their firearms—something Brakes had hoped they wouldn't need, but the situation now demanded it. As they headed out of the station, the evening air was cool, the sky tinged with the deepening hues of twilight.

The drive to the outskirts of town was quiet, the air thick between them. The radio crackled faintly with updates about possible German air attacks, but none of it registered with Brakes. His mind was fixed on the installation—what lay there, hidden for years, and why it had suddenly become so crucial.

The narrow country road they followed soon became rough and uneven. Vera navigated the car with skill, but the closer they got to the coordinates, the more isolated and desolate the landscape became. Trees lined the road, their dark branches stretching over them like skeletal fingers. The gravel crunched under the tires as they turned onto a smaller, barely visible path that led to the installation.

"We're getting close," Vera said, her voice cutting through the eerie quiet.

Brakes strained his eyes; he could see something emerging out of the darkness. "This should be it. Vera, stop the car"

They quietly retrieved their stuff and headed down the overgrown path. It opened into a large clearing, and there it stood: the remnants of the military installation, hidden in the shadows of the woods. The building was old, with crumbling walls and boarded-up windows, a relic from a time long forgotten. Its eerie silhouette stood against the fading light, almost as though it was waiting for them.

"Looks abandoned," Vera remarked, her tone carrying a note of unease.

"Looks can be deceiving." Brakes muttered, opening the door and stepping in.

Vera followed. Both moved quietly as they surveyed the building. The air was frigid, and the wind whispered through the smashed windows, giving the whole place a haunted feel. Brakes' hand hovered near his gun, ready for anything.

A faint smell of rust and decay permeated the rooms. They stepped into what seemed to be an old administrative office, papers strewn across the floor, desks overturned, and filing cabinets long since emptied.

Brakes gestured for Vera to follow as they moved deeper into the building. Every sound—their footsteps, the creak of old doors swinging in the draughty spaces—felt unnaturally loud in the oppressive quiet.

They found a staircase leading down into a lower level. Brakes paused at the top, shining his torch down into the darkness. "This is where it'll be," he said, his voice low.

"Whatever it is," Vera added, her grip tightening on the flashlight in her hand.

They descended carefully, the steps groaning under their weight. At the bottom, a long, narrow hallway stretched before them, lined with metal doors. Most were rusted shut, but one door at the far end stood slightly ajar, light flickering from within.

Brakes exchanged a glance with Vera. "Be ready; someone is here."

They approached the door cautiously, with Brakes reaching out to push it open. The room beyond was a stark contrast to the decay above. A single flashlight tied overhead illuminated the space, casting harsh shadows over the walls. In the centre of the room stood a metal table, and on it lay several objects: blueprints, documents, and what appeared to be a small metallic device, no bigger than a briefcase.

Brakes stepped forward, his eyes narrowing as he inspected the papers. "These are military schematics," he said, flipping through the documents. "Blueprints for some kind of weapon. A prototype."

Vera was about to respond when a sudden noise behind them made her spin around. The door slammed shut, and they both drew their guns instinctively.

Out of the shadows, a figure emerged. It was a man. He was tall, wearing a dark overcoat, his face obscured by the dim light.

"Well, well, Inspector Brakes. You really are like a dog with a bone, aren't you." The man said, his voice cold and shrewd.

Brakes' grip tightened on his gun. "Who the hell are you?"

The man stepped forward, just enough for the light to catch his face. It was someone Brakes didn't recognise, but the cold intensity in his eyes, the way he held himself and his speech patterns extruded a strong person of high standing. Brakes saw everything he needed to know—this must be the person Kingsley had been working for.

The man smirked, glancing down at the blueprints on the table. "This little secret of ours was supposed to remain hidden. You've meddled where you shouldn't have."

Vera aimed her gun at the man, her finger hovering over the trigger. "I suggest you put your hands where we can see them."

The man's smile only widened. "I think it's a bit too late for that, don't you?"

Before Brakes or Vera could react, the man knocked the flashlight down from its lofty place. Darkness swallowed the room, and amidst the chaos, Brakes heard a sharp thud followed by Vera's gasp.

"Vera!" Brakes cried, but a blow to the back of his head sent him reeling to the ground, and everything went black.

Brakes awoke sometime later with a pounding headache, his vision blurred as he tried to focus. The room was still dark, save for a faint glow from the flashlight laying on the floor. Brakes tried to move, only to find he couldn't.

His hands were bound tight behind him, his body left on the cold concrete floor. As he struggled to get up, Brakes realised that Vera was behind him, still unconscious but breathing.

It was quiet. Too quiet, Brakes realised as he looked around desperately, only to quickly realise that he and Vera were now the only people in the room.

The man was gone and so were all the blueprints.

CHAPTER EIGHTEEN

Brakes' head throbbed as he struggled to get his bearings. The cold concrete pressed against his cheek, and he forced himself to focus. Vera's shallow breaths beside him were a small relief—she was still alive, at least. But they were in serious trouble. Their hands were bound behind them, and the room's eerie quietness was only disturbed by Brakes' struggles.

"Vera," Brakes whispered hoarsely, nudging her with his shoulder. "Vera, wake up."

She stirred slowly, letting out a groan. "What... happened?" She muttered, her voice thick with confusion.

"They got the drop on us," Brakes replied grimly, pulling at his restraints. His wrists were tightly bound with some kind of thick wire, cutting into his skin on his right wrist as he moved. The left one, still bandaged, was throbbing like hell due to the pressure on his broken wrist. He glanced around the room. The door was still shut, and there was no sign of the man or men who had ambushed them. "We need to get out of here."

Vera blinked, shaking off the fog in her head. "Damn it... that hurts." She winced as she tried to sit up. "My first murder case, not even a copper and already I have been shot at and tied up twice. Not sure I am cut out for this, sir."

Brakes nodded with a sigh. "I understand, Vera. It's my fault for letting you help, but we'll get out of this," Brakes reassured her, his eyes scanning the darkness. "We might have walked into a trap, but they've underestimated us."

With a grunt, Brakes twisted his body, trying to find anything sharp in their surroundings that could cut the wire. His eyes landed on a piece of broken glass not far from where he lay, the remnants of some long-forgotten bottle. If only he could reach it…

"Vera, try to shuffle closer to that glass over there. We can use it to cut these restraints." Brakes urged softly.

Vera, still groggy, nodded weakly and began awkwardly shifting her body across the floor. The movement was painful and slow, but finally, her fingers brushed against the shard. She grabbed it as carefully as she could, struggling to manoeuvre her wrists while avoiding cutting herself.

Brakes moved closer, turning his back to her. "Get mine first."

She nodded, her hands shaking slightly as she began to saw through the wire binding Brakes' wrists. The sharp edge of the glass bit into the wire, and after what felt like an eternity, it snapped free.

Brakes exhaled in relief, quickly undoing the rest of his restraints. Without a word, he turned to Vera, cutting her loose in return. She flexed her sore wrists and looked at him, her expression tired but determined.

"What now, sir? How is that wrist of yours?" Vera's gaze swept over Brakes, her mouth curling into a frown. "Look at you, beaten and broken but still going. Just how do you do that?"

"You get used to it, Vera." Brakes sighed. Then, almost belatedly, he realised something felt off. Looking around the dark room, he narrowed his eyes. "Have you seen my hat?"

Vera's eyebrows pinched together. "All this, and the only thing you care about is that bloody hat," she muttered, though there was a hint of humour to her words.

Brakes stood up slowly, testing his balance. His head still spun, but there was no time to dwell on it. "We need to find that man and stop him before he disappears with whatever those drawings are."

Vera nodded, rubbing her temples. "Well, if nothing else sir, at least we are still breathing."

Brakes carefully opened the door and peered out into the dimly lit room. "Grab that torch over there. Look for another one and my hat, Vera, please."

The building was silent. They had been left behind, likely deemed too incapacitated to be a threat. That was their only advantage now—the element of surprise. Soon, Gray would be arriving, too, and that wasn't a reunion Brakes was looking forward to having.

Moments later, Vera tapped Brakes on his shoulder, handing him his pistol, hat, and a torch.

"Let's move," Brakes whispered, leading the way.

They crept through the remaining parts of the building, looking for any further signs of what had gone on here while every step echoed ominously in the quiet space.

They reached the end of the hallway, and Brakes pushed open another door, revealing a larger room—what appeared to be an old storage area. The dim light flickered overhead, casting long shadows across the stacks of rusted crates and forgotten equipment.

Brakes paused, his senses on high alert. There was a slight noise, almost imperceptible, coming from the far corner of the room. A faint scraping, like someone moving something heavy.

He motioned for Vera to stay low as they edged forward, keeping to the shadows. As they rounded a stack of crates, Brakes spotted movement. It was the man from before, his back to them as he hunched over a cylindrical object.

From what Brakes could see, it looked to be long, large and made of metal. He was running his hands over it, almost reverently, his breath coming in sharp bursts of admiration.

The object was clearly something special. It had to be at least six feet in length and at least four feet in diameter. No wonder if was left behind—the thing must have weighed tonnes.

Brakes crouched behind a crate, gripping his gun tightly. "We've got him."

Vera nodded, her eyes narrowing in focus.

"Stay here." Brakes whispered. "I'll circle around and get behind him."

Vera gave a quick nod, positioning herself for a clear line of sight. Brakes silently moved around the perimeter of the room, keeping low and using the crates as cover. The man remained oblivious to their presence, still fixated on whatever he was looking at.

When Brakes was close enough, he stood and levelled his gun at the man's back. "Don't move."

The man froze, his hands still on the object. Slowly, he raised his arms in surrender, but his voice was calm, eerily so. "You're too late, Inspector."

Brakes didn't lower his gun. "Vera, get something to tie this bastard up with, will you." Brakes yelled into the darkness. The man simply looked at Brakes smugly, his smile cruel despite the gun poised to shoot him.

"You think you've won something here, Inspector?" He chuckled, though his eyes were cold. "It doesn't matter what you do to me now."

Brakes kept his gun trained on him. "Who the hell are you?"

The man's smile widened. "You'll find out soon enough. But by then, it'll be too late for you, for everyone. The plans are already on their way to Germany."

Vera returned with something to bind the man's wrists. Standing behind him, she took his pistol and started tying his wrists together. Before either Brakes or Vera could react, however, the man broke away from Vera's grasp and lunged at Brakes.

Vera fired instinctively, but the man was quick—too quick. A deafening explosion ripped through the room, sending Brakes and Vera crashing to the floor as the blast rocked the building.

Brakes' ears rang, and the world around him blurred. Dust and debris filled the air, and for a moment, everything fell into chaos. He struggled to push himself up, coughing and disoriented, his gun lost in the debris.

"Vera!" He shouted, trying to see through the haze.

A hand grasped his arm, and he turned to find Vera pulling herself up beside him. In the dim light, Brakes could see blood trickling down her forehead, but she was thankfully alive.

"He... he set off a charge." Vera coughed, her voice strained.

Brakes staggered to his feet, his heart pounding. The man was gone, the room destroyed in the blast. Rubble and metal now formed a large pile in the centre of the room, a monument that signified Brakes' failings.

MI5 were not going to be happy, he realised with a shudder.

"We need to get out of here," Brakes said, coughing through the dust. The building creaked ominously now that the structure had been weakened by the explosion.

Reaching for Vera, they stumbled toward the exit as the walls groaned around them. Outside, the cool morning air hit them like a wave of relief, but Brakes' mind was spinning.

The man had escaped. The device—whatever it was—was likely gone or destroyed.

As they caught their breath, Vera looked at Brakes with a grim expression. "Let's get out of here before Gray arrives, sir."

Brakes wiped the dust from his face, staring out into the dusk lightened forest. "No. We regroup and figure out just who the hell that is," he said, his lips twisting into a frown. "Because if that man was telling the truth, something worse is coming, and we're the only ones who can stop it."

Brakes and Vera stood by the car in the dim light outside the crumbling building, the weight of the explosion and their failure hanging heavily between them. The air was thick with dust, mingling with the faint scent of oil and damp earth.

Nothing about this felt right anymore—the stolen plans, the Marsh family, and now the mysterious men in dark suits. One was dead in the cells, while the other had escaped. It was all connected, but exactly *who* was pulling the strings?

"Sir, you know a little about engineering," Vera began, referring to Brakes rebuilding his bike while she watched the after-effects of their crumbling operation. "Do you know what it was that we saw in there?"

"That is well beyond my scope, Vera." Sighing, Brakes shook his head and turned to his comrade. "Truly, I have no idea. All I know is that thing is now destroyed, and the plans are gone."

Vera wiped a streak of blood from her forehead with the back of her hand and glanced at Brakes. Despite the exhaustion behind her eyes, there was also a sense of resolve about her.

"We need to tell Gray, sir. We can't keep chasing shadows," she said quietly, and Brakes knew that she was right. "That blast back there could have killed us."

Brakes nodded, rubbing the back of his neck. He didn't want to tell Gray, of course, but sooner or later, he would have to. That, or have Gray eventually find out himself.

"You're right. But we can't go to Gray. Not yet. I want this man, Vera; he is mine. If the Marsh family's influence stretches as far as I think, then there's no telling who we can trust."

Vera frowned. "Then what do we do? We can't just wait for them to make the next move."

Brakes gazed out into the distance, the wind rustling through the darkened trees. The moon hung low in the sky, the sun just breaking the horizon, casting an eerie glow over the countryside. They had been on the back foot for too long. It was time to switch tactics.

"We go back to the source," Brakes said, his voice resolute. "Ann Marsh. There's something we've missed—something that she isn't telling us, that ties all of this together. I'm certain of it. She knows everything and everyone involved."

Vera's eyes widened. "You think you can get that out of her?"

"She is spent, Vera. She knows it, too," Brakes said. "We don't know the full scope yet, but if anyone holds the key to unravelling this mess, it's the Marsh's.

"It won't be easy, sir. Look how long it took for her to divulge the existence of the notebook." Vera shifted her weight, her boots crunching against the grass.

"We'll see about that, Vera. Back to the station."

The two of them set off, retracing their steps through the woods and back to the main road. The morning air was cold as they got in the car, but the adrenaline pumping through Brakes' veins kept him warm. His mind worked furiously, replaying everything that had happened so far. The deaths, the ambush, the stolen plans, and the man's cryptic warning about it being *"too late."*

By the time they reached the outskirts of Norwich, the sun had fully risen and was bringing some much-needed brightness to Brakes' and Vera's world.

They arrived at the station, and as Brakes got out of the car, he suggested that Vera return home and clean up. She readily agreed and sped off, leaving Brakes standing outside the front of the station. The wind, although slight, blew the dust and debris from his suit. Brushing himself off, he turned and headed inside.

After cleaning himself up a bit in the men's room, Brakes went to go find the Chief so that he could bring him up to speed on the developments of the case.

He did not make it to the Chief. As he made his way through the swing doors that divided the public and police areas, Brakes immediately stopped in his tracks when he saw that Gray and several other men were waiting for him at his desk.

"Just what the bloody is hell is going on, Brakes?" Gray spat, his eyes cold as he stared Brakes down. "We arrived at the coordinates, only to find a pile of rubble and dust. And by the looks of you, you have been there, too."

Gray cast a discerning look over Brakes' suit, the flecks of dust and debris still clinging to it, like damning evidence. Brakes grimaced and took a step forward, ready to fight his case, only for Gray to bellow over him.

"Arrest him!"

Brakes blinked over at Gray, completely dumbfounded. "Arrest me?" He asked, unmoving as two men made their way over to Brakes and pulled his hands behind his back. "For what, exactly?"

"Let's see," Gray hissed, and lifted a hand as his men cuffed Brakes. "Destruction of Government property, failure to follow orders, espionage." He ticked off each offence on his fingers, stepping closer to Brakes with every word.

Finally, he stopped in front of the detective until they were practically nose to nose.

"And that's just the start." Gray said, his voice low and dangerous. He turned back to his men. "Take him to the interrogation room."

CHAPTER NINETEEN

The tension in the air was electric as Brakes was placed in handcuffs and led off to an interrogation room. Then, as if to taunt Brakes, the Chief chose that exact moment to enter the room.

"What's going on?" the Chief asked, a flash of annoyance crossing his face as he looked between Gray and Brakes. "Unhand my man immediately."

"Sorry, Chief; I outrank you." Gray smirked. It was clear that he was enjoying this. "And besides, this comes from the top—From Churchill himself."

The Chief's eyes narrowed. "We'll see about that. I'm coming in there with him." He threw off his overcoat and followed the men as they pushed Brakes into the interrogation room.

The two men forced Brakes down into the chair where the arrested usually sat. He felt like a criminal and, not for the first time since being cuffed, he considered whether he should have simply listened and waited to go to the military installation with Gray that morning.

Though he felt slightly disorientated, Brakes was still fully aware of one of the men grabbing hold of his hat and slamming it down onto the table. It looked crumpled, now, and though he said nothing, Brakes shot a dark glare at the man.

Gray dropped down in the seat opposite Brakes, and was swiftly followed by the Chief, who turned to Gray with a scowl.

"Well? Come on, then. This is *your* shit show," he growled, motioning over to Brakes before finally turning to him. The Chief's voice grew softer. "You'll be fine, Brakes. This is all a misunderstanding. Clearly, *someone* somewhere has their wires completely crossed."

All Brakes could manage was a roll of his eyes and a shake of his head.

Over the course of the next hour, Gray sat and grilled Brakes while the Chief listened in silence. There was no emotion on his face, but it was clear that he was unhappy with the situation. Brakes offered little, instead choosing to hang his head low while Gray spat angrily in his direction.

"This gung-ho attitude of yours will *not* be tolerated anymore, Brakes," Gray hissed, banging a fist against the table. "If you continue down this path of self-destruction, you can and *will* be held responsible."

Brakes could only nod meekly in agreement. It was a point that the Chief had brought up consistently in the past, one Brakes had ignored in favour of 'following the trail'. Yes, he was completely aware of his own misgivings, but he did it all for the sake of doing what was right. Could they not see that? Brakes' mouth curled up at the corner as he lifted his head to finally meet the Chief and Gray's eyes.

"Alright, alright. No more one-man band stuff," Brakes groaned, tired as he finally admitted defeat. "From now on I will act as a part of this team. You have my word." His lips twisted into a grim line and started squirming in his seat. "Now, can you get me out of these bloody cuffs? Then we can finally get to the brains behind this conspiracy before they do any more damage."

Gray shot the Chief a disbelieving look, but the Chief thankfully nodded in Brakes' favour before getting up to leave the room. With a ragged sigh, Gray turned back to his men and ordered them to release Brakes.

"Bring Ann Marsh to interrogation." Gray instructed one of the constables while Brakes, finally uncuffed, rubbed his sore wrists and stood up to stretch his legs. Rolling his shoulders, Brakes picked up his hat and took a quick walk around the room while Gray kept a careful eye on him.

Minutes later, the Chief called Brakes into his office. Thankful for the momentary reprieve from Gray's discerning gaze, Brakes immediately took his leave and entered the Chief's office, promptly closing the door behind him.

The Chief was sitting at his desk, his hands folded on top of the polished surface. Disappointment flickered in his eyes, and Brakes felt his superior's dismay deep within his bones.

"Despite your best efforts, I must make you aware that your most recent misconduct and arrest will now become public record," the Chief explained, his tone grave. "Your file will be updated by morning."

Brakes could only nod as silence settled between them. Then the Chief sighed heavily, the sound resonating within the room.

"You can't afford any more black marks on your record, Brakes," the Chief said, his voice low. "You need to start playing by the book. Next time, you could lose your job, or worse—you could end up in jail."

Brakes stiffened, realisation finally settling upon him. The Chief was right; if he didn't start following the rules, he would be no better than the criminals that graced their cells. In fact, he *would* be one of them.

Before Brakes could reply, a constable knocked on the glass panel of the Chief's office door. They both looked up, and the constable entered to inform them that Ann Marsh was ready.

"Thank you," the Chief nodded, standing up from his desk. "Well, Brakes? Let's go." And without another word, the Chief walked out of his office with Brakes hot on his heels.

They found Gray waiting for them both at Brakes' desk. His arms were folded across his chest, his face set with determination as he watched Brakes and the Chief walk towards him.

"Well?" he asked, clearly displeased with the turn of events. Brakes shrugged, and the Chief simply chose to get straight to the matter at hand.

"This time, all three of us will go in there," the Chief said, his voice booming across the room. "Enough is enough; we will intimidate this woman as much as is required. We must finish this *now*."

Without another word, Gray and Brakes followed the Chief into the interrogation room. Ann sat there, smaller than Brakes remembered. It took a moment for her to react when the door slammed shut, but when she turned to look up at them her eyes were wide and gaunt.

Slowly, the three of them made their way to the table until they were towering over Ann. She shrank back in her seat and began to tremble, submissive in stature as she cowered beneath their penetrating gaze.

"Now, listen here, Marsh," Gray snarled, planting both hands on the table. "You're most certainly going to hang; treason is a crime most unforgiving, as you well know. But maybe—just maybe—we can help you, but only if you help us."

Gray watched Ann for a second before pulling back. His gaze was unwavering as he stepped away from the table, allowing a hollow silence to permeate the air. Ann watched him, the tremors in her body only seeming to increase as she waited for Gray's next words.

Finally, after a minute of agonising quiet, Gray spoke again, his tone calm but firm.

"We need to know everything, and this time, don't you dare leave a single thing or person out," Gray instructed, a promising threat laced into his words. "This is truly your last chance to save your life."

Ann Marsh shook her head, tears beading in the corners of her eyes. "You can't stop these people. They have too much power," she whispered, her voice small. "Even more power than Churchill."

Brakes and the Chief exchanged a look, their eyebrows rising. Gray, on the other hand, looked at her incredulously.

"I highly doubt that," he sneered. Ann shook her head again, this time a little more weakly.

"It's true. This goes much higher, way past that of our prime minister."

"You're talking about parliament figures?" Brakes asked in disbelief. Ann sighed and rolled her eyes.

"No, no, *no*," she snapped, her eyes finally meeting Brakes'. "Much higher. Think more along the lines of Royalty."

A stunned silence fell over the room this time. The Chief, Gray and Brakes all exchanged a look, each of them unsure how to process the news. If Ann was right, then this truly was bigger than any of them had ever anticipated.

Finally, the Chief stepped forward, his face twisting into something dark and threatening as he stalked over to Ann.

"You can't be serious? You're telling us that the King and his family are behind this? You have lost your mind, woman!" The Chief yelled, his face growing red with rage. Turning to a constable, the Chief pointed an accusing finger toward Ann. "Take her back to the cells! I refuse to listen to any more of her stupidity!"

Without a word, the constable took Ann by the arm. She didn't put up a fight, but once she was at the door she stopped and turned back to face the three of them again.

"The King and his immediate family are not the only Royals in Britain," she said, choosing her words carefully. Gray simply arched a brow, unimpressed.

"Is that all?" He asked. A beat of silence passed between them. Then Ann smiled knowingly, the tiredness entrapped within the lines of her face transforming into something akin to amusement.

"Look, I cannot say much, but I can tell you this." Taking a deep breath, Ann looked between the Chief, Gray and Brakes, confidence now burning in her voice. "There is a meeting tonight. At an abandoned barn just outside of the city. If you go there, you will meet with a man. The same man that we have dealt with from the beginning."

Ann smirked, watching as confusion and disbelief bloomed on each of her interrogators' faces. "He is certainly of high standing. Well-educated, finely dressed, and whenever he mentioned the man that he works for, he would always refer to him as 'His Grace'." Then she was stepping out of the room, her final words echoing in the quiet room. "Like I said: Royalty."

And then she was being pulled away, led back to the cells while the three men looked between each other in quiet disbelief. When the door swung shut and Ann Marsh's footsteps fell away, Gray finally let out an exasperated exhale and shook his head. Brakes started to pace the room, throwing his hands up into the air while the Chief slumped down in a nearby chair, his head falling into his hands as he mumbled to himself, muttering incoherent and jumbled words to himself.

It took a couple of the minutes for the men to regain their wits. Once they did, Brakes turned to his superiors and, tiredly, asked what he considered the most important question in that moment:

"Tea, everyone?"

Slowly, they made their way out of the interrogation room one by one and quietly gathered around the teapot in the common area. As Brakes poured them each a mug of steaming tea, they pondered over this astounding revelation. Gray took a measured sip from his mug once Brakes handed it to him.

The clock ticked, deafening against the quiet before Gray finally spoke up.

"Right, fellas. Now is not the time to cock this one up." His voice was gravelly, his words daunting. Gray then turned to Brakes and looked at him pointedly. "No one man bands. It will not be just us and you lot, either. This is going to be a joint operation from now on. These people will not get away from us. Not this time.”

Brakes offered a weary nod. “What’s the plan, Gray?” He asked, gripping the hot mug between his palms.

Before Gray could begin to explain further, Vera barged into the room. When she saw the three men gathered together, each of them wearing identical expressions of concern, surprise flashed across her face.

“What’s going on?” She asked innocently, her eyebrows arching in anticipation.

No one replied. Instead, both the Chief and Brakes turned to Gray, waiting for his answer. After what felt like hours, Gray finally cleared his throat and broke the silence.

“Okay. Chief, get every man and woman you have, officer or not, I don’t care—just have them assemble in the front of the station in thirty minutes. My men are already waiting outside with our trucks,” Gray instructed, his tone stern as he stared at the Chief. “We are going to this meeting tonight, together. We will completely surround the place so that not even a rat will be able to escape.”

The Chief nodded, his back ramrod straight. “Yes, sir,” he replied, and immediately went to call on all the officers and constables within the station. Gray finally turned to Brakes and Vera.

"You two," he said, his brow furrowed. "Go down to the holding cells and let the officers know what we are doing. Time is of the essence, after all." And with that, Gray turned on his heel to go talk with his men, leaving him and Vera alone in the common area. Vera simply turned to look at Brakes, her eyes swimming with questions.

"What on earth happened while I was at home, sir?" She asked. Brakes could only sigh, his mind and body weighed down by the events of the day.

"I will explain everything, Vera," he murmured, putting down his mug of tea. "But first, let's do as we have been told. Come along."

They made their way down to the holding cells and, as briefly as he could, Brakes explained what had happened during Vera's time at home. She was shocked by all that had transpired, however that soon gave way to excitement as Brakes instructed the cell officers to join the others at the front of the station. As they made their way back upstairs, he could practically feel Vera vibrating with anticipation behind him.

Thirty minutes later, the station was now only manned by a single cell officer while everyone else had piled into their respective cars. The Chief had taken a seat in Vera's vehicle as Brakes slid into the backseat, his nerves practically singing as Gray turned to everyone, his gaze hardened.

"Man your vehicles and follow us!" He cried, his voice booming against the quiet of the day. Then he slipped into his own car, the engine roaring to life.

One by one, cars trickled out of the station and slithered onto the roads, the hum of each engine a dangerous purr amidst the everyday noise that thrummed within Norwich.

The journey took a little over twenty minutes, but it felt more like a lifetime as the cars crawled down the road. Soon, they turned round a corner and found themselves driving down an overgrown path, long forgotten in the throes of war.

There, looming menacingly ahead stood the barn, weathered with age and swallowed by shadows. Vines clung to the outer walls and crept into its broken windows, as if holding it up long after it had been abandoned.

One by one, each car crawled to a quiet stop some feet ahead of the building and, as silently as they could, everyone stepped out of their cars, their weapons at the ready.

They tip-toed toward the barn until officers and Gray's men were practically shoulder to shoulder, their backs pressed against sun-bleached walls or crouching underneath cracked windows. No one dared to breathe as they surrounded the place in a tight circle, their chests rising steadily while Brakes, the Chief and Gray readied themselves and made their way toward the door.

Brakes' heart thumped heavily against his chest, his pulse rushing as his nerves rose. He turned to look at Gray, his brows set in determination and waited for his signal. Finally, after what felt like an hour, Gray slid his gaze across to Brakes and gave a small, identifiable nod.

"*Go*," he mouthed, and Brakes did not need to be asked twice.

They burst through the door, their weapons drawn. The wooden structure groaned painfully under the sudden movement. In the darkness, two figures turned sharply. One seemed to be holding a handful of papers, while the other shadowy figure held a briefcase. In the dim light, Brakes watched them freeze and their eyes grow wide with shock.

"Police! Hands where I can see them!" Brakes bellowed, his voice commanding in the dark space.

The man with the papers raised his hands slowly, but his eyes darted to the various exits, calculating an escape. The shadowy figure, now fully illuminated by the weak morning light, was younger than Brakes had expected, well-dressed with a gaunt face and a thin moustache. He, too, raised his hands, but there was something off in his comportment—an unsettling calm.

"Drop the briefcase. And you, drop those papers and step back," Brakes ordered the two men. His gun stayed trained on them both, unwavering. A crooked grin spread across the second man's face, his posture unnervingly perfect.

"You're too late, Inspector," he said in a low voice, the words slipping out like a taunt. "It's already in motion; these are simply loose ends. You have stopped nothing."

Brakes felt a chill crawl up his spine. He didn't like where this was going.

"What's in motion?" Growled the chief, his own grip tightening on his pistol. "Speak clearly, or I'll make sure you won't have the chance to—"

Suddenly, a loud, metallic clatter echoed from the back of the barn. Brakes spun around just in time to see the man who had been holding the paperwork bolt for the side exit. No one bothered to go after him. There was no need; he was running right into a trap.

During the momentary distraction, the refined man had reached inside his coat and pulled out a small pistol.

Brakes dove to the side just as the man fired, the shot ricocheting off the wall behind him. The wooden planks splintered, dust flying everywhere. Brakes rolled behind a stack of crates, firing two shots in quick succession. The bullets whizzed past the man's head, forcing him to duck behind a pillar.

"Give it up!" Brakes shouted, reloading. "You're not getting out of here alive!"

"Listen to the inspector. You have no chance," the Chief yelled, now crouching a few feet away from Brakes. "There are three of us in here, all armed, plus about twenty or more people surrounding the building outside. You have nowhere to go."

The man didn't respond. Brakes could hear him moving, inching closer to the back of the barn. In the dim light, Brakes could make out an old ladder that led up to a loft. The man was trying to gain higher ground. Brakes needed to end this fast.

Crouching low, Brakes moved silently along the side of the barn, keeping his eyes trained on the man's shadow as it shifted along the wall. The moment he saw the man's foot hit the first rung on the ladder, Brakes took his chance.

He fired again, the bullet slamming into the wood just inches from the man's leg. The man staggered, nearly losing his balance, but he recovered quickly and scrambled up the ladder.

Brakes cursed under his breath. "Why don't they ever bloody listen."

Climbing the ladder after him, Brakes reached the loft just as the man swung the briefcase like a club. Dodging the blow, Brakes grabbed the man's arm and twisted it behind his back. The briefcase fell to the floor below with a thud.

"You've got nowhere left to go," Brakes growled, wrenching the man's arm tighter. "That's enough, now; let's go."

"It's all for nothing, don't you see?" He hissed, beginning his descent down the ladder. "What do you think you're stopping? It's already been done." He continued climbing down, now under the watchful gaze of Gray and the Chief, both with their pistols trained on the man.

"What are you talking about? What's already been done?" Brakes snapped, his own pistol still trained on the man.

The man gave a hollow chuckle, his eyes wild. "As I mentioned, these are simply loose ends. I was just going to burn them. You see, we don't need them; all the required information has already been dispatched. Weeks ago, in fact."

His grin only seemed to widen, confidence rolling off him in waves as Gray made his way toward the entrance to call for a couple of uniformed officers. Even as they placed their latest suspect in handcuffs, his smile never seemed to waver. He even had the gall to look amused while the Chief grabbed the briefcase from the floor and chuckled menacingly when Brakes began gathering the paperwork that the man's accomplice had strewn across the barn floor.

Gray stalked over the entrance, his expression unreadable. "Take him back to the station," he ordered, watching as the man was led out of the barn. "Everyone else, thank you for your hard work and efforts. You may stand down and head back to the city immediately."

With that, Gray turned back to the barn and nodded toward Brakes and the Chief, who were looking over the paperwork with a mixture of intrigue and trepidation. Once they were certain all the officers had left, the three of them retreated from the barn and made their way back to Vera and the car.

Outside, the sun had fully risen, casting a warm glow over the countryside that felt jarringly out of place compared to the tension of the last few hours. Brakes took a deep breath, trying to shake the unease creeping into his chest.

Back at the car, Brakes placed the briefcase on the bonnet while the other two men started passing around the paperwork they had been looking over. Running a hand through his hair, he looked between the Chief, Gray and Vera before allowing himself a heavy sigh.

"Let's take a look at what that toff has in here."

Brakes knelt down, his fingers working at the lock. With a few deft motions, he popped it open, revealing stacks of documents, maps, and what appeared to be a set of blueprints for something mechanical.

Vera peered over his shoulder. "What is that?"

Brakes sifted through the papers, his eyes scanning the intricate designs. "I'm not sure yet," he muttered. "But whatever it is, it's what they've been protecting all along."

He pulled out a small photograph from the pile. It was a grainy black-and-white image of what looked like some kind of engine, similar to the one from the factory. Except this one looked as if it were in full working order, flames emitting from the back of it. Beside it stood a man in a lab coat, his face partially obscured. But Brakes could see enough to recognise him.

It was Sir Frank Whittle, engineer and inventor.

Brakes' blood ran cold. The pieces were finally starting to fall into place, and the picture they were forming was far more dangerous than he had ever imagined.

"We need to return to the station," Brakes whispered, looking between the ashen faces of the Chief and Gray. "Now."

CHAPTER TWENTY

The drive back to Norwich was tense, the weight of the briefcase sitting heavy in the back seat. As the quiet countryside passed them by, Brakes took the time to bring everyone up to speed on exactly who Sir Frank Whittle was.

"Whittle is the co-inventor of the turbo jet engine, but he was turned down by the government for funding and development aid," Brakes explained, earning a nod from both the Chief and Gray. "Recently, he completely lost his mind, but Whittle has continued with his research and, judging by the photo found in this briefcase, he seems to have actually got the engine to work."

"The material shows that Whittle has not been able to get as far as fitting the engine to an aircraft yet," Gray supplied. Of course, Gray and MI5 would be aware of who Whittle was, too, Brakes thought. "And if what our suspect has said is true, then that means that the Germans now hold the blueprints for the world's first working turbo jet engine."

"It doesn't help that they also have some of the world's best scientific minds," Brakes said, his tone grim. "It will not take them long before they have a fully operational jet aircraft, and that will surely change the cause of the war both in the skies above and on the ground."

The rest of the journey was spent in silence, the weight of what they had uncovered pressing down on them all. Once they were back at the station, Gray took the briefcase and paperwork with him and headed straight for London; their findings needed to immediately be reported to the highest level of MI5.

The only thing that was left to do was interrogate their latest prisoners about *who* was behind all of this, and if it was, in fact, a member of the Royal family that Ann Marsh had hinted at before. That was all they needed to know—after all, Brakes already knew why two people had died, and that a major espionage ring had been uncovered in the midst of John Marsh's murder case.

Of course, Brakes was keenly aware that he hadn't stopped anything, but at least the higher powers would be fully informed and made aware of what was possibly to come in the near future.

For now, however, both Brakes and the Chief agreed that it was for the best to let the two men sweat it out in the cells for a while. Breaking for lunch, the Chief returned to his office, most likely to call the higher ups about their latest development within the case, while Brakes and Vera made their way out of the station for some well-deserved respite.

They sat together in Brakes' favourite café near the market, enjoying a nice cup of tea with lunch. They chatted idly together while watching the world go about its business until it was time to head back to the station.

Vera went back to her car alone upon Brakes' request. This allowed him a slow, thoughtful meander back to the station as he contemplated the questions he would ask the prisoners. Of course, only one question seemed pertinent to the investigation: Who was the person behind all this? It was the only piece of information that might be able to shed some much-needed light in the dark, devious world Brakes had found himself entangled in.

By the time he had walked through the station doors, Brakes had decided he would take a crack at the streetwise gent first. Of the two, he seemed to have more to lose than the stiff-upper lipped toff sat in the adjacent cell. Calling for one of the officers to bring the man up to interrogation, Brakes strode over to his desk for a moment to think over his questions, and to give the man some time to think over his actions and what the outcome might be.

Ten minutes later, as Brakes entered the interrogation room, he knew he had been right; the man was terrified, his face pale and his eyes rimmed red while he cowered in his seat. It seemed the thought of hanging for treason had played its part in the past few hours.

Brakes didn't even get a single word out. The moment the man saw him, he started bargaining with Brakes in a bid for his safety.

"Look, I'm not hanging for this. If I tell you everything I know, can you help to spare me from the noose?" He asked.

Brakes contemplated the man's plea, but only for a moment. "Tell me what you know. It's not up to me regarding your sentencing, but I could make a recommendation; it all depends on your candidness here today," replied Brakes.

The man hesitated, and Brakes considered if he would say anything. Then, the suspect started singing like a canary, and the melody was truly beautiful.

"He keeps everyone at arm's length. He thinks the only person who knows who he really is, is the toffee-nosed twit you arrested with me. But I know him. I know all about him," the man said.

"Stop messing me about," Brakes insisted, quicky becoming exasperated. "Just get on with it and give me his name."

"Leopold Charles Edward George Albert. He's a prince, part of the Royal family," the man said, his voice trembling as he spoke the name. "He develops spy rings for the Germans, who then go on to steal, kill and a whole manner of other stuff, all for him. Everything ends up in his hands. He then sells it to the Germans, or in some cases simply passes it on." The man's confession tumbled out of him with ease, however his voice grew to a whisper the more he spoke, his breath growing shallow.

Once he was done, the man had devolved into a quivering mess. His hands were clammy, and his hair plastered to his forehead with sweat. Brakes' eyes grew wide, and he turned to the uniformed officer standing by the door.

"Bring the other prisoner up," he murmured to officer. "And take this one back to the cells."

Without another word, Brakes got up and left the room. Even as the door swung closed behind him, Brakes could still hear the man's desperate pleas for mercy, but that was now out of Brakes' hands. All he had needed were answers, and once he confirmed the name with the toff, he was certain that he would finally have them.

It did not take long for his second suspect to be brought up, and once he was safely secured in the room, Brakes entered to find the toff staring right back at him with a smug, self-assured smile fixed to his lips. It seemed that, unlike his babbling associate, this man had not been the least bit affected by his time spent down in the clink.

Brakes was certain that that confidence would not last long, however.

"Does the name Leopold Charles Edward George Albert ring a bell?" Brakes asked. There was no point in beating around the bush—if he was going to get *this* canary to sing, too, then Brakes would have to go straight for the jugular.

And it did the trick, because the moment that name left Brakes' mouth, the toff's smile slipped and he turned white as a sheet, as if he had just seen a ghost.

"H-How…" He started, but Brakes simply lifted a hand to silence the prisoner.

"I wouldn't worry about how I know," Brakes said, his voice dangerously low. "What you *should* worry about, however, is *what* is going to happen to you. Now, tell me what you know."

There was a moment where the toff held Brakes' gaze, his lips pressed into a thin line as if he were going to take the secrets to the noose with him. Then, with a shuddering breath, the toff broke.

"Yes, yes, I know him. He is our employer," he revealed, his voice quiet. "He is the one that provides targets for assassinations, information to steal. He is the one that orchestrates it all."

It did not take long to extract the remaining information needed from the toff—further plans, exactly what their boss had been chasing, and more. Once he was done, Brakes nodded over to the waiting officer and made his way out of the room, leaving the toff to sit in defeated silence.

Brakes quickly returned to his desk and called Gray on the telephone. The answer was immediate.

"They have given me a name," Brakes breathed, his voice low. "Leopold Charles Edward George Albert. Do you have anything on him, Gray?"

There was a pause on the line. "Wait one moment, please." Gray finally said, and the phone hovered silently next to Brakes' ear for what seemed like an eternity. Beside him, Vera had appeared and leaned up against his desk, curiosity in her gaze.

Moments later, the Chief emerged from his office and parked himself close by, eager anticipation for what might come next rolling off his body. Brakes' jaw tensed; he had not anticipated having an audience during his call with Gray.

Finally, there was a noise on the end of the receiver. It was muffled at first, then the clear sound of pages turning on the other end of the telephone.

"So?" Brakes asked, growing impatient. "Do you have anything on the man, Gray?"

Gray sighed heavily before answering. "I have in my hands a file, about two inches thick. It seems that this man is already well-known to us," he replied, his voice heavy. "He is certainly a Royal Prince, but he is also a German Duke and, at one point or another, a sitting Nazi politician. We currently have him residing in Berlin."

Brakes blinked, stunned into a momentary silence. He looked between Vera and the Chief, both eagerly waiting on him to update them with bated breath, before turning back to the phone.

"So, that's it then, Gray?" He asked, feeling a touch aggravated. "He is untouchable?"

Another sigh sounded from the receiver. "I wouldn't say that, exactly, but I will certainly have to pass this up to the chain of command." There was another pause, as if Gray were contemplating his next words, before he continued. "For what it's worth, congratulations, Brakes—you finally got your man, in a manner of speaking."

And then he put the phone down, leaving Brakes with the hollow quiet at the end of the phone.

Brakes put the receiver down and turned to find the entire room watching. It seemed like all eyes were on him. Taking a deep breath, he took a moment to gather his thoughts before finally bringing everyone up to speed.

As he spoke, everyone listened with bated breath while he recounted the events of the day, what the two suspects had said, and what Gray had told him regarding Leopold Charles Edward George Albert, the Royal Prince and German Duke.

When it came to his verdict, however, it felt as if everyone in the room began to deflate. Brakes couldn't blame them, of course; it felt anti-climactic, and even Brakes hadn't expected how little even MI5 could do in this situation.

Everyone dispersed quickly after that. The Chief, however, walked over to Brakes and clapped him on the back.

Sixteen "Well done, Brakes; as usual, you didn't give up." The Chief said, his voice almost cheerful as he gave Brakes a stiff nod. "Although you haven't had the chance to actually slap cuffs on the man, you can rest assured that, if he ever shows his face on British soil again, he will most certainly hang."

And with that, the Chief took his leave and made his way back to his office. Brakes groaned with relief and, now that all eyes in the room were no longer on him, he finally sank into his chair as Vera came to stand beside him, her eyebrows arched.

"It's finally done, isn't it, sir?" Vera asked.

Brakes nodded. "It is. But in this line of work, it never really ends."

Vera gave a small, weary smile. "At least for today, it does."

"Let's get a pint, hey," he said, turning to Vera with a rare smile. "I could use a different type of headache right now."

She chuckled to herself. "I'll get the car." Vera said and began walking away.

Brakes grabbed his coat and hat, giving it one last re-shape before placing it back on his head. "You've been through it the last few weeks, haven't you?" he muttered to himself, tenderly brushing the rim before throwing on his coat and making his way toward the swing doors.

The case was now closed, and with it, a chapter of Brakes' life. There would undoubtedly be more mysteries and crimes, but for now, Brakes could finally have a rest.

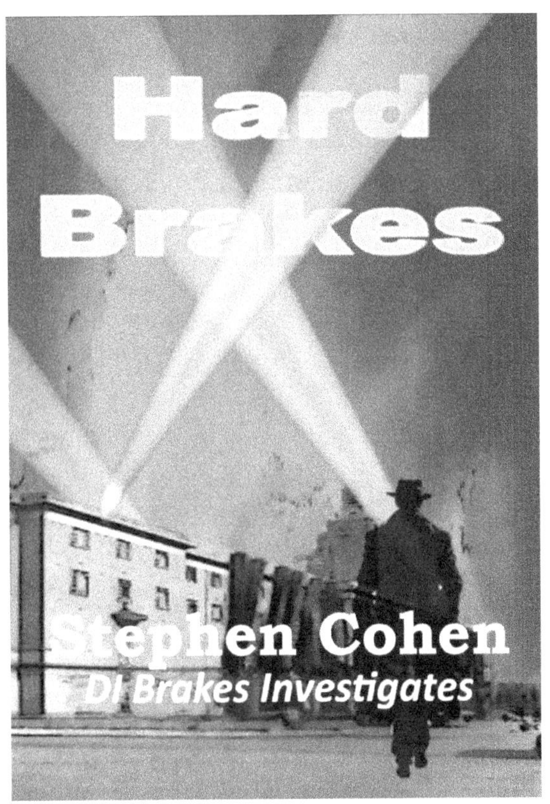

*Now you can read an excerpt of **DI Brakes Investigates – Book 2 Hard Brakes** in this WWII crime fiction series, **COMING SOON**.*

CHAPTER ONE

The year was 1942. England's rolling countryside, once a picturesque symbol of tranquillity, had become a landscape marred by war. Bomb craters pockmarked the earth, homes stood in ruin, and the nightly wail of air raid sirens was a constant reminder that death could come from the skies at any moment. Yet, amidst the terror brought by German bombers, there was another shadow creeping across the land, one more insidious and perplexing than any enemy aircraft.

It was a darkness that Detective Inspector Brakes had spent three long years chasing in-between other cases—five bodies, five deaths, each one more inexplicable than the last. His case load, although varied at this time, had nothing to offer him. Each case felt dull and boring, part of the everyday grind and crime that was now war-torn Britain.

And after the lacklustre end to his previous case some months ago, Brakes was simply itching for something to reignite his passion for the chase, and he was certain this case could do exactly that. So, for the first time in months, he unboxed his nemesis.

Brakes sat at his kitchen table in his modest cottage home, staring at the wall in front of him. Plastered across the cracked, faded wallpaper were newspaper clippings, police reports, and photographs, all detailing the five victims who had been found in various locations across the English countryside over the past three years. Each time, the bodies were discovered dressed in different military uniforms, parachutes attached but never deployed. There was something grotesque about the pattern, something that gnawed at the edges of Brakes' mind, refusing to let him rest.

"Five victims, five parachutes. The only links: parachutes, not deployed. Military dress," he muttered, rubbing his chin as he scanned the clippings for the hundredth time. His words bounced off the silent walls, offering no reply.

His home reflected the mind of a man consumed by his work. Every available surface was cluttered with papers, books, and remnants of his investigation. In the corner of the room lay his trusty, half re-assembled Triumph Speed Twin 5T, his beloved 500cc motorbike that Brakes had been restoring after his accident last year.

Initially, it was housed in tangled pieces in the garage, but recently Brakes had needed an easier direct approach, so he moved it into his living room. It had been his one retreat from the madness of war and crime—a place where his hands could focus on something tangible, something that made sense. But the Triumph had gone untouched for weeks now, unloved and gathering dust while the metal lay bare, as his mind remained locked in a different kind of conundrum.

The victims of the cold case had been scattered across the country, their bodies discovered in the most unlikely of places—open farmland, dense forests, rivers, even on top of abandoned bomb shelters. What troubled Brakes most was that, apart from one—an RAF aircraft mechanic—none of the victims had any apparent connection to the military or aviation. Yet there they were found, dressed in military attire, with parachutes strapped to their backs, as if they were part of some sort of military covert exercise that went tragically wrong.

Well, if that was in fact the case, then the mission was doomed from the start. In all five files, not one pilot had given a statement, nor had they been found.

The cases had baffled local police, and with the nation's attention on the war effort, these deaths were quickly written off as accidents or errors in parachute deployment. In each case, the medical examiners had concluded that the victims had died from injuries consistent with a high-velocity fall. Their parachutes had failed to open, with the fall killing them on impact.

Brakes winced at that thought. Falling through the sky, desperately pulling at the static line in a last desperate attempt to deploy the chute, only for it to not open. Watching the ground below inching closer and closer, knowing what was about to happen. What goes through someone's mind in this situation? The terrible anticipation of death had to be all-consuming.

Just the mere thought of it sent a chill through Brakes, and his entire body gave a prolonged shudder. Closing his eyes, Brakes forced himself to go through the motion as if he had been there, too.

Had it been night or daytime? They must have been alone. Apart from the pilot, that is, otherwise surely, someone would have come forward. Then, they jump out of the aircraft. But wait—why weren't they using a static line parachute? Immediately, they reach behind to open the cute.

It does not open.

They try again, blood rushing through their veins like volcanic lava as their heart starts beating faster and faster. They're plummeting through the air at over one hundred miles per hour, and sheer panic finally sets in.

They start to sweat, grasping at the static line and pulling, pulling, pulling, to no avail. Sweat begins to pour from their body, so much so that not even the fast-flowing air can dry their skin or clothes. Tears begin to sting their eyes, and realisation hits.

They are heading to their doom.

Immediately, they squeeze their eyes shut and hold their breath as they await the inevitable.

Brakes opened his eyes and immediately headed for the kitchen sink. Splashing some water over his sweat-laden face, he grabbed a flannel and soaked it under the tap. He headed off to his room to change his shirt, making sure to wipe himself down before putting on a fresh one.

What were their final thoughts, Brakes wondered? Was it the fear of what would become of them once they hit the ground, or their loved ones who awaited their return? Sitting down on his bed, Brakes placed his head in his hands and groaned softly.

"Don't do that again, you idiot," he mumbled to himself, moments before a fresh chill ripped through his body.

Heading back downstairs, he buttoned up his shirt whilst casting his eyes back over the evidence in front of him.

Brakes wasn't convinced these cases were separate incidents. Something didn't sit right with him. Why would ordinary civilians—people who had no business being near aircraft or airfields—be found dead in such a manner?

Brakes sighed, falling back in his chair and rubbing his tired eyes. He had been working on these cases unofficially at home for three years now, gathering whatever scraps of information he could in his spare time. His superiors had little patience for his theories, dismissing the deaths as nothing more than tragic accidents. But Brakes' gut told him otherwise. He had been in this line of work long enough to know when something was wrong, and this case had a stench to it, like that of a rotting vegetable lost behind a kitchen cupboard.

His eyes wandered to the old clock on the mantelpiece, its third hand ticking away steadily toward sunrise. He hadn't slept much, his mind too restless to allow for such a luxury. As the first rays of daylight crept through the narrow window above the sink, Brakes stood up and stretched. The cold remnants of last night's tea sat in his cup, but he downed it anyway, savouring the bitter taste.

"Time to see the Chief," he muttered to himself. Heading into the bathroom, Brakes cleaned himself up and readied himself for the day ahead. Pulling his coat from the hook by the door, Brakes slipped it over his dark blue suit, grabbed his hat and opened the door to the early morning chorus of bird song and engines roaring in the distance.

Brakes' timing was perfect; Vera was just pulling up to his house, ready for another day at the station.

Though Brakes' injuries had fully healed from his accident several months prior, the medical officer had yet to sign him off as fit to drive, which meant that he still relied on Vera to drive him around due to his lack of progress on the Triumph.

This had not been the case for the past few weeks, however, as Vera had been on a training programme to officially join the team. Instead, Brakes had to tolerate one of the most introverted constables from the station as his stand in driver. The lad was a stark contrast from Vera and, at one point, Brakes would have relished in his presence. But truth be told, over the past few weeks, Brakes had found he now missed Vera's intense desire for interference.

"Morning, Vera," Brakes said, opening the car door. "Nice to have you back."

"Morning, sir. It's good to be back," Vera grinned, puffing out her chest proudly. "And in my proper uniform, at last."

Brakes couldn't help but smile, pride swelling in his chest. "Welcome to the force, Vera," he said, and slid into the seat beside her. "I always knew you would make a great addition to our team. Congratulations."

"Thank you, sir." Vera beamed, her smile wide. "And now that I am an official constable, I won't keep getting told to wait in the car or to stop asking questions."

As the words left her mouth, Vera shot Brakes a playful, accusatory glance, and he felt his cheeks grow warm. Clearing his throat, Brakes slammed the car door shut behind him.

“You still might have to make the tea though, Vera,” he grumbled, taking his hat off and placing it on the dashboard. “Do try to remember that it’s your first week, though. Take things slow, learn the craft.” The last part was said encouragingly, earning Brakes a genuine smile from Vera.

As they made their way through the quiet streets of Norwich, Brakes couldn't help but feel the tension creeping into the air. The war had changed everything. The city was no longer the peaceful place it once was. Instead, it had become a maze of ration lines, bomb shelters, and crumbling buildings. Fear was palpable, and it wasn't just the threat of Luftwaffe bombers that hung over the city like a dark cloud.

There was a sense that the very fabric of society was unravelling. People were desperate—rationing, shortages, and constant uncertainty had taken their toll. And now, with the unexplained deaths, it seemed that even the ground beneath their feet wasn't as solid and unsoiled as it used to be.

DI Brakes Investigates – Book 2 in this WWII crime fiction series is coming soon. Use the following link to sign up for my newsletter, release dates, un-released facts and more: -

https://books2read.com/author/stephen-cohen/subscribe/1/207713/

You can also find me on Linktree, social media links, subscribe and follow me: -

https://linktr.ee/stephencohen

A personal note from the author:

Thank you for reading book 1 in my new crime series. Please don't forget to leave a review, follow and subscribe to my channels and newsletter, to keep up to date with upcoming new releases.

Thank you for your support.